KV-277-193

DEADLY PURSUIT

When New York businesswoman Jackie O'Hara finds out that she's terminally ill, she must put her affairs in order, and top of her list is making peace with her estranged brother Danny. But Danny, sole witness to a high-profile gangland murder, is on the run from the Russian Mafia. Jackie begins her worldwide search for Danny knowing she's in a race against time. However, she could surprise everyone and live for years — or she might die today, or tomorrow.

Books by Steve Hayes
in the Linford Mystery Library:

A WOMAN TO DIE FOR

With David Whitehead:
FERAL
DEAD END
FANATICS
KILLER SMILE
UNDER THE KNIFE
CAST A DEADLY SHADOW
TOMORROW, UTOPIA
BLACKOUT!
NIGHT CREATURES

STEVE HAYES
AND ANDREA WILSON

DEADLY
PURSUIT

Complete and Unabridged

LINFORD
Leicester

First published in Great Britain

First Linford Edition
published 2013

Copyright © 2012 by Steve Hayes
and Andrea Wilson
All rights reserved

British Library CIP Data

Hayes, Steve, *1930 or 1931* –
Deadly pursuit. - -
(Linford mystery library)
1. Suspense fiction.
2. Large type books.
I. Title II. Series III. Wilson, Andrea.
813.5′4–dc23

ISBN 978–1–4448–1509–2

SWINDON
BOROUGH COUNCIL
LIBRARIES

Set by Words & Graphics Ltd.
Anstey, Leicestershire
Printed and bound in Great Britain by
T. J. International Ltd., Padstow, Cornwall

This book is printed on acid-free paper

Part One

1

My name is Jacqueline Bonjour O'Hara.
It's a mouthful, so most people shorten it
to Jackie O'.

I own JB&O, a boutique advertising
agency in Manhattan that due to my
being a workaholic, has become prosper-
ous enough for me to buy an old but
elegant six-story condominium building
on West 12th Street overlooking the
Hudson. I live in the penthouse. It has
views of New York to die for and my one
big gripe in life is that because of the
competitive nature of my business I don't
spend as much time there as I would like.

I was driving home from the annual
Manhattan Businesswomen's Award Dinner
thinking exactly that thought and promising myself for the zillionth time to do
exactly what my staff keeps nagging me to
do — not work so damned hard — when I
saw the accident.

It was at the intersection of West 12th

and 7th Avenue. A tank-sized Lincoln Navigator had plowed into an old Toyota Corolla with Minnesota plates, crunching it with such force that the car was squashed. It must have just happened because there were no police or paramedics present — only a few curious onlookers, one of which was a tall young guy in jogging clothes. He was on his cell and I guessed he was calling 911. But he was on the far sidewalk, out of earshot, and in case he wasn't I pulled over and called in the accident myself.

That should have been the end of it. But as I finished the call I saw the head and shoulders of a little girl poking out of the broken rear window. No more than six, she wasn't moving and her face was lacerated by broken glass. The man and woman slumped over in the front seat — presumably her parents — had been crushed by the head-on impact and appeared to be dead.

Jumping out of my vintage 356 Porsche Speedster, I ran to the Corolla. I smelled gasoline and looking down saw a puddle of it forming by my feet. Fearing that the car might explode any second, I peered in through the rear side-window. The harness the child had been strapped in had broken away from the seat, allowing her to be hurled through the rear-window. I looked closely at her pale, blood-streaked face. There was no sign of life. I guessed she was dead, but ever the optimist decided to check for a pulse anyway. I pressed my finger against her neck. Nothing! I pressed harder. Still nothing! I was about to give up when suddenly I felt it, pumping feebly.

Thank you, Moses!

I straightened up and listened, but could hear no wail of approaching sirens. It wasn't surprising. Traffic in Manhattan always moves like it's stuck in molasses, but on Saturday nights it resembles a jammed parking lot. It could be another ten minutes before the paramedics arrived. By then, I reasoned, the little girl might be dead.

I couldn't let that happen. Against all better judgment, I grasped her by the shoulders. Voices all around me kept telling me not to touch her. I ignored them and gently pulled her out through the shattered window. Cradling her against me, I blew the wisps of butter-colored hair from her face and silently begged her to open her eyes. She didn't. She didn't move either. She just lay limply in my arms. Hoping that I wasn't too late to save her, I started back to my Porsche. That's when I heard someone yell 'fire!'

I didn't wait to see where it was but sprinted toward my car. It was only about twenty yards away and I jog five miles every day on my office treadmill, but something told me I wasn't going to make it. Protecting the little girl with my body I threw myself to the ground, rolled over twice and made it to the space between the rear of my Porsche and the car stopped behind it — just as the Corolla exploded.

The explosion momentarily deafened me. Then flaming debris began crashing down everywhere. People were screaming. From under the rear of my Porsche I saw shadowy shapes, silhouetted against the burning Corolla, darting back and forth across in front of me.

I looked at the little girl still cradled in my arms. As I did her eyelids fluttered open, revealing frightened blue eyes. Without thinking, I jumped up, ran to the driver's side door of my car and yanked it open.

2

St. Luke's-Roosevelt Hospital Center, on West 12th Street, was a minute's drive from the accident — unless, like tonight, there is traffic. Then it can take forever. Honking continually and ignoring all the rules of the road, I raced down 7th Avenue toward 11th, cut in front of a stopped taxi and turned right on Greenwich. Traffic there was equally heavy, forcing me to weave around cars and roar through a yellow light until finally I skidded to a stop in the hospital driveway.

Grabbing the limp little girl from the now-blood-soaked back seat, I squeezed between two parked ambulances and hurried into Emergency. The would-be patients huddled on chairs in the waiting room looked up as I burst in. I rushed to the nearest admissions window and told the sour-faced staffer hunched over her computer that I needed a doctor right away. She gave me one of those patented withering 'wait your turn' looks and continued typing.

I lost it. 'My little girl's dying!' I screamed at her. 'Get me a doctor now or I swear to God I'll spend every last cent I've got making sure your sorry ass is fired!'

Unfazed, she went on typing.

Whether by Fate or coincidence a doctor suddenly pushed out through the swing-doors. I rushed up to him, begging him to help me. He responded the way you'd hope a doctor would respond under such circumstances: he told me to follow him and elbowed open the door for me.

He led me to a screened-off bed in the E.R. There, he examined the child and asked me how she'd gotten hurt. I quickly explained. He called a nurse over and told her to get X-rays taken and to determine the child's blood type in case she needed a transfusion. 'Oh, and while you're at it, nurse, take her mother, here, to admissions and have her fill out all the necessary paperwork.'

'I'm not her mother,' I began. But he'd

already turned back to the little girl. Giving the nurse a shrug, I followed her to admissions.

Since I wasn't connected in any way to the child, there wasn't much paper-work to fill out. But while I was waiting in reception for the doctor to return, two police officers entered. They spoke to the sour-faced staffer who pointed at me, and then came over and began questioning me about the accident.

'There's nothing I can tell you about it,' I said. 'It happened before I got there.'

The older of the two officers, a man pushing thirty, checked his notes before saying: 'Witnesses claim you refused to wait for the paramedics.'

'What paramedics?'

'The paramedics that arrived right after you grabbed the kid and ran off.'

'I didn't 'run off,'' I said angrily. 'I couldn't hear any sirens coming, so I drove the little girl over here. Oh, and by the way, did any of your so-called 'witnesses' happen to mention that the car blew up just seconds after I pulled her out of the rear window?'

'No need to be sarcastic, lady,' the young female officer said. 'We're just doing our job here.'

'Then do it without making me seem like a criminal for trying to save a little girl's life!'

Her partner said something to her that I didn't hear. She nodded and left. 'All right,' he said, taking out a pad and pen, 'I need to make out a report. May I see your driver's license, please?'

His tone sounded ominous.

'Maybe I should have my lawyer here,' I said, reaching for my Blackberry Bold.

The officer sighed like his feet were hurting. 'In that case, lady, tell him to meet you at the station house on West 10th, 'cause that's where you'll be making it.'

'Excuse me . . . '

I looked up and saw it was the doctor. 'How is she?' I asked quickly.

'Hanging in there. But she needs a transfusion. Trouble is she has a fairly rare type of blood, Type B positive, and we're out of it. I've got a nurse checking around to find out which hospital or

11

blood bank has any — '

I cut him off. 'No need to do that, doc. That's my blood type. I'll gladly give her some of mine.'

The doctor looked at the officer. 'Your report will have to wait.' To me, he said: 'That'd be great. Come with me and we'll get a sample of your blood to make sure it's compatible.'

I got to my feet, started to follow him then looked back at the officer. 'What about the parents? Did they make it?'

The officer shook his head.

I sagged. My mother died just before my fifteenth birthday and my dad passed away two years later. I still miss them both dreadfully, but at least I knew them long enough to know they loved me. This little girl had barely gotten to know hers and now they'd been snatched from her; and as I accompanied the doctor into the E.R. I wondered if I'd done her a favor by keeping her alive.

3

I knew there was something wrong by the doctor's grave look when he re-entered the room where earlier the nurse had drawn my blood.

'Damn,' I said softly. 'She didn't make it, did she?'

'What? Oh, no, no, she'll make it . . . '

'Then . . . ?'

He hesitated — never a good sign when you're talking to a doctor — and said: ''Fraid I have some bad news.'

'Don't tell me — the cop in the waiting room wants to arrest me for kidnapping?'

'It's a little more serious than that.'

His tone was as grim as his expression. Though it was hardly the time, I looked him over. He was hot. Dark eyes, a bedside smile and thick brown hair I wanted to run my fingers through. 'All right, doc. Let me have it.'

'It's your blood, Ms. O'Hara — '

'Please, call me Jackie O' — '

'We're testing it again to make sure there's no mistake, but — '

'Mistake?' A cold, clammy lump settled in my stomach. 'Mistake about what? Wait a minute,' I said before he could answer. 'Are you saying I've got something wrong with me?'

His tight-lipped silence suggested he did.

'Cancer?'

'CML, actually,' he said quietly. 'Chronic myelogenous leukemia.'

Stunned, I couldn't make my lips work for a moment. 'But you could be mistaken?' I said finally. 'I mean, labs do make mistakes, right?'

'More often than we'd like, yes.'

'But in my case you don't think they did?'

'Let's say, I think you should see your own doctor right away.'

'That's no answer. Give it to me straight.'

Instead he sighed wearily, the expelled breath fluttering his lips.

'Dammit, doc! You must have an opinion. Let me hear it.'

'As a doctor, I try not to rely on my opinions, Ms. O'Hara. I find it better all around if I just stick to facts.'

'And the fact is, doc, you think I've got CNL whatever it is — '

'CML.'

'CML — CNL — CNN — what the hell difference does it make. It's obviously serious and you think I've got it. I can see it in your eyes.'

'It would seem so,' he admitted. 'But as you said, labs do make mistakes and I advise you not to get too stressed out until we know for sure.'

I wasn't listening. There was a roaring in my ears and my skin crawled. 'Question?'

'Go ahead.'

'If I do have this CML, is it curable?'

He hesitated and now I knew I was in deep trouble. 'At present, there is no known cure. But there are drugs known as tyrosine-kincase inhibitors or TKIs that when taken daily will keep you alive.'

'For how long?'

'That depends. Each patient is different — '

'Cut the crap, doc. How long?'

'Two years, give or take.'

Two years! I went numb. I felt the examination table under me start shaking. I glanced down and realized it wasn't the table; it was my knees.

'I'm very sorry,' the doctor said.

'Me, too.'

'You mustn't give up hope, Ms. O'Hara. New cures are discovered every day and — '

'Shut up,' I told him. 'Just shut up and let me think.'

4

Jeanine, my ex-husband's sickeningly loyal assistant, ushered me into his office and assured me that Mr. Harmon would be with me in a moment. I thanked her, envied her gym-hard ass, waited until she closed the door behind her and then did what I always do when I enter Kirk's office: stood there on the pearl-gray carpet marveling at the panoramic view of New York City. Like the view from my penthouse it was breath-taking. But this evening, as I looked at the glittering lights, I hated it.

I'd already had several martinis, but decided I needed another. So wading through the ankle-deep pile I went to the bookcase holding all his law books and pressed the button hidden under the third shelf from the top. Silently, the bookcase split in half to reveal a mirrored wet bar. As I reached for the bottle of Kauffman Luxury vintage vodka, which resembled a curved, silver-topped decanter, I saw the exquisite red rose lying beside his business card. I smiled, despite my depressed mood, knowing what the note would say even before I read it.

'I made extra in case you were thirsty. Love, K.'

I opened the small refrigerator and sure enough, there sat a pitcher of vodka martinis beside a chilled glass and a jar of green olives stuffed with bleu cheese.

I could have cried.

Pouring myself a martini, I took the pitcher, red rose and jar of olives over to the large glass-topped desk and sank gratefully into a black-leather executive chair. The rose smelled heavenly. I stuck it in the pitcher in case it needed a drink like I did. Then picking up my glass I took a long gulp. As the cold, cream-and-honey nectar drained down my throat, I leaned back and gazed about me. Kirk's office isn't as large as an aircraft carrier — though it looks like it when you enter — but he's rich enough to buy one.

I've never been one hundred percent sure how he makes his money. When we were married a few years back and at a party or some political function, I remember people asking him what he did for a living. He would smile mysteriously, as if it were a secret, and reply: 'I'm a lawyer of sorts.'

And for some reason, maybe because he was so tall, so damned charming and boyishly-distinguished, no one ever questioned him further. Not even me.

Now, as I drained my glass and quickly refilled it, an inner door opened and Kirk strolled in. Dressed entirely in pale gray, his signature color, he was an ad for Zegna!

Three long strides brought him beside me. He leaned down and I smelled something expensive on his dark stubble as he kissed me lightly on the lips.

'Mm-mmm, you taste yummy!'

Normally I would have had a cute comeback. Not tonight.

'Oh, man,' he continued wearily, 'am I glad to see you, Irish.'

'Bad day?'

'The worst.'

'I'll share my martinis with you.'

'I might just take you up on that.'

He was joking, of course. Kirk's a health nut who doesn't drink anything but water, juice and vitamin drinks and it was my cue to laugh. But I couldn't even manage a chuckle.

'You too, huh?' he said, noticing.

'The pits.' I gulped down my martini.

Planting himself on the edge of the desk, he loosened his silver-gray tie and took my hands in his, said: 'Talk to me.'

Ever since I'd left the E.R., I'd been trying to think of the best way to tell him about my condition. Despite our divorce, or maybe because of it, I still loved him. Just as importantly, I admired and respected him, and knew he felt the same about me. Most people, especially our friends, cannot understand why we ever got divorced. The answer is complicatedly simple: something in our DNA brings out the worst in us, making it impossible for us to live together. But even though we argue about almost everything, we would never deliberately hurt each other. Not for any reason. Which is why as I looked up into his deep-set, gray-green eyes, I was surprised to hear myself blurt:

'I'm dying.'

'That calls for another pitcher of martinis.'

'I'm serious.'

'So am I.'

Then, abruptly, I was crying.

That caught his attention. In the four-and-a-half hectic years we were married, no matter how furiously we argued he'd never seen me cry.

'Oh God,' he said softly. He squeezed his brows together. 'Oh, no, Irish, not you, kitten . . . no . . . no . . . that can't be right.'

'My words exactly.'

★　★　★

He pulled himself together and stood tall. 'We must get a second opinion. And a third and a fourth, if necessary. I mean this has to be a mistake.'

'It'd be pretty to think so.'

Suddenly he was angry. 'Jeanine!' he yelled. 'Get in here!'

If she'd twitched her nose she couldn't

21

have entered faster. 'Yes, sir?'

'Get me Charlie Dunstan at Johns Hopkins. Tell him unless he's doing a bone marrow transplant on the President, I want to talk to him.'

'Yes, sir.' She started out then turned back to him. 'About anything in particular, Mr. Harmon?'

Kirk looked questioningly at me.

'CML,' I said.

He must have known what the letters stood for because he sagged and for a moment closed his eyes.

'Just get him,' he told Jeanine wearily.

5

The next morning at Johns Hopkins Dr. Charles Dunstan's 'second opinion' turned out to be equally grim: a complete blood count test verified that I did indeed have CML. And though a daily diet of imatinib or nilotinib capsules would prolong the inevitable, he doubted if I would live more than eighteen months.

'The doctor at St. Luke's-Roosevelt gave her two years,' Kirk said.

'I hope he's right,' Dr. Dunstan replied gently. 'In fact I hope she lives until she's a hundred — which, I might add, is entirely possible.' He smiled fatly across the desk at me, adding: 'You do understand, my dear, this is guesswork at best. In the thirty-odd years I've been a hematologist, I've had patients who by all rights should've died within a few months live into ripe old age — while others, people I expected to be senior citizens, were gone in a heartbeat.'

'Thanks,' I said numbly. 'I'll do my best to prove you're wrong.'

★ ★ ★

We flew back to New York in Kirk's private Lear jet. A despicably curvy, sweet young blonde in a light gray Donna Karen suit with a blinding white smile asked if we'd like refreshments.

'Do you mind if I get hammered?' I asked Kirk.

'Not so long as I can get drunk with you.'

'Idiot. You don't drink, remember?'

'I do now.'

'Ho ho ho.'

'Ask Holly, here. She'll tell you. Go on, Holly, tell her. Tell how much I drink these days.'

'He passes out regularly,' Holly said, smiling.

Kirk tried to convince me with one of his serious looks. 'I've changed a lot since you divorced me, Irish. Now I get smashed every night.'

'Ho ho ho,' I repeated. Then: 'And I

didn't divorce you. We both agreed that divorce was the only way we'd survive.'

'Exactly! That's why you can't die on me, Irish. I'd have nothing to live for. Make us a pitcher of vodka martinis, please,' he added to Holly.

'Did you buy her that smile?' I asked as she walked away.

'I can't remember. No, honestly,' he said before I could jump on him. 'All my employees have health insurance, dental too, so it's possible that indirectly I — '

'Are you doing her? Or can't you remember that either?'

He looked hurt. 'You know my rule: never with employees.'

'That is one of the lamest excuses you've ever come up with.'

'Lame or not, it's the truth.'

We both stopped talking as Holly returned with our martinis.

'You have awesome teeth,' I told her. 'Did you go to Mr. Harmon's dentist to have them capped?'

'Yes,' she said, smiling. 'How did you know?'

'Just a wild guess.'

'Did you go there too?'

'No,' I said sweetly. 'Free dental work was one of the few items I didn't include in our divorce settlement.'

'That was cruel,' Kirk said as Holly lost her smile and fled back to the galley. 'Cruel and unkind. Not like you at all.'

'Sorry,' I said. 'I know it sounds selfish, but I'm having a hard time dealing with this dying business.'

6

We didn't speak again until we were seated in the back of the limo, driving away from Kennedy. Then Kirk asked me if I'd heard from Danny.

I shook my head. 'Not a peep.'

'Shit head.'

Much as I wanted to, I couldn't disagree with him.

'I know he's your kid brother, Irish, and I know you hate it when I bad mouth him, but for once you have to agree with me: this time he's really outdone himself.'

'He's older now,' I said, trying to keep it light. 'Had more practice.'

'Yeah, and never an ounce of discipline.'

'What was I supposed to do — beat him with a baseball bat whenever he did something wrong? Judas, he would've been black and blue all over.'

'Might have served him better than having you constantly coddling him.'

'Fuck you!'

'Nothing like a snappy comeback.'

'Anyway, I didn't coddle him.'

'No, you just made excuses for him every time he screwed up. Hell, it's no wonder the kid was in trouble every five minutes. He knew his big sister would be there with an open check book and a bleeding heart to bail him out.'

'Well-thank-you-Dr.-Phil!' I glared at him in the plush, leather-smelling luxury of the limo. But the coward wouldn't look at me; he just kept his eyes fixed on the traffic outside the window. 'You know, Kirk, you're very big at judging other people — '

'I'm not judging.'

'Criticizing, then.'

'Not criticizing either. And even if I were, your brother deserves it.'

'Let's not go there, all right?'

'Ducking his responsibility to the D.A. — disappearing without a word — then hacking into your bank account — you, the one person who's bent over backwards to love him and treat him fairly all his life. I mean, good God, Irish, isn't there anywhere the little jerk draws a line?'

'If there is,' I said angrily, 'you're hardly the person to point it out to him!'

'What's that supposed to mean?'

'Well, you ain't exactly followed the straight and narrow yourself, have you?'

'Oh, for Pete's sake!' Kirk threw up his arms in exasperation. 'Don't start in with that crap again! How many times do I have to repeat that I'm not fronting for or tied in with the Russian Mafia in any way, shape or form?'

'Till I believe you, I guess.'

'Believe what you want! You will anyway. That's your problem.'

'My problem?'

'But I guarantee you this, Miss Jackie O' — no matter what I have or haven't done, or will do in the future I've never stooped low enough to steal money from my own sister!'

It was hard to argue with him. When my brother, a misfit in everyday life but a genius when it comes to computers, electronically transferred a hundred thousand dollars from my business account to a local B of A then promptly withdrew the money and took off for parts unknown, it not only shocked and enraged me but had caused a lingering hurt that I wasn't sure would ever go away.

'I'm not saying what Danny did wasn't wrong,' I said after a long pause, 'or that I forgive him for it. But at the same time, you and I weren't under the kind of pressure he was. After all, the D.A's office and the police promised to protect him from any kind of mob retribution if he testified against Dmitri Kazlov — and what happened? A lousy hit-man tries to gun him down as he leaves the court-house — and that was only after testifying before the Grand Jury. I mean, good grief, is it any wonder he didn't want to stick around for the actual trial?'

Kirk was silent for so long I wondered if he'd been listening to me. Finally, he pressed his hands fondly over mine, said gently: 'Let's not beat each other up over this anymore, okay? We've got a far more important issue to worry about right now. So let's concentrate on that.'

'Fair enough. So where do we start?'

'First thing you need is a game plan.'

'Sounds like you've already got one.'

'Just some ideas.'

'I'm listening.'

'Well, the first item on the agenda should be the agency and what you're going to do with it.'

'That's easy. I'm going to sell it.'

He frowned, surprised. 'That was a quick decision.'

'From now on, chum, speed is the name of the game.'

'All right. So the agency's sold. Then what?'

'I'm going to find him.'

'Him?'

'Danny, of course! If I'm going to die soon, as the doctors seem to think, then I want him to know.'

'Why?' he asked.

''Cause he's my brother — '

'Who couldn't care less about you — or anyone else!'

'He's still my brother. And conscience dictates I have to tell him.'

'First you have to find him.'

'I've got two years to do that.'

31

'I wouldn't count on it.'

'Thanks.'

'I didn't mean it that way. I meant Kazlov — he's no doubt got men out there intending to ice Danny even as we speak.'

'All the more reason I should start looking right away. On top of that,' I added, 'this guy I know in the D.A.'s office says he's heard that if Danny somehow skips the country then Interpol will look for him, too.'

'Interpol? Why would they get involved? He's not a terrorist or a big-time international criminal.'

'Doesn't matter. My friend says it's some kind of courtesy thing — you know: one law agency helping another.'

Kirk sighed. 'Well, much as I think you're wasting valuable time, you know I'll help you all I can.'

'That goes without saying, Mr. K.' I leaned close and kissed him on the cheek. 'But I still love you for offering.'

He chuckled grimly.

'What?'

'I just had a thought. Don't suppose

you'd consider remarrying me?'

'Thanks, but I'm already dying fast enough.'

'That's not very friendly.'

'No,' I said. 'But neither's asking your ex- to marry you again when you're wearing another's woman's perfume.'

'What?' He looked alarmed.

'It's all right,' I laughed. 'I'm just kidding.' But I wasn't. He smelled of Chanel Number 5 — the same fragrance worn by Holly when she'd served us martinis during the flight.

7

Not surprisingly, I got no sleep that night. Much as I tried to convince myself that I might be one of the rare and lucky people who survive fatal diseases, the cold hard realization that that was probably just wishful thinking wouldn't go away. On top of that I couldn't help wondering if I even wanted to survive knowing that from now on my life would be one of uncertainty, of never knowing for sure if I would see tomorrow — of traipsing back and forth to doctors' offices for blood tests and medications that if they were anything like chemotherapy and radiation treatments made you feel sick and miserable. And God only knew what the side-effects might be!

Frazzled and depressed by burgeoning negativity, I got up shortly before dawn, fixed myself a Bloody Mary and sat at the window facing the Hudson. Below, the trees lining Henry Hudson Parkway glistened with dew. The river glinted like pewter. A perky sparrow landed on my window ledge and nibbled at the crumbs I always leave out. Normally I would have enjoyed its company. But today I rapped on the glass, chasing it away. I watched as it flew out over the river, all the while envying it its freedom, then angrily told myself to stop feeling so damned sorry for myself and headed into the bathroom.

I should have had a hangover. But I rarely get hangovers, and other than being raw-eyed from staring at the ceiling all night, I felt no ill-effect from my martini binge. After a hot shower I put on my favorite jeans, an old Sting concert T-shirt and shoe-boots, washed down my vitamins and supplements with a glass of O.J. and left for the office.

Knowing you might die within two years drastically impacts your goals and brings ultimate clarity to your thoughts. During the night as I lay there weighing what few options I had left, I'd decided not to sell my agency but to put it into the more-than-capable hands of my vice president and most-trusted friend, Dana Sheridan. That way, I reasoned, I could devote all my time to finding my brother and still have something to fall back on if I lived longer than expected.

JB&O is located on the 6th floor of an 80's high-rise facing east, only a few minutes from my condo building. I've been there almost five years and as if to verify how little social life I had, Wesley, the security guard, didn't even pretend to be surprised to see me at six-thirty in the morning.

''Nother day, 'nother dollar,' he said mechanically as I passed him.

I wanted to say that nothing could be further from the truth but instead I mentally flipped him the bird and rode the elevator up to the agency.

Dana was already at her computer when I breezed into her office. At thirty-seven, she was vivaciously pretty, had the body of a gym rat and always looked annoyingly immaculate. This morning was no exception. 'Hi, boss,' she said, not looking up. 'Just getting home from a hot date?'

'Cute,' I said. 'It so happens I had a rough night.'

'So that's why you look like something the dog dragged in.'

'I think you mean cat.'

'No, you look worse than that.'

'Thanks. Did I mention you're fired?'

She laughed. 'Why so early, anyway?'

'I wanted to talk to you. Alone.'

'Uh-oh,' she spun her chair around and looked at me. 'Did we lose the Vogue account?'

'It's worse than that.'

'Kirk conned you into remarrying him?'

'Shut up and listen,' I said. Pulling her to her feet, I dragged her over to the couch and told her everything. She was too shocked to interrupt me and by the time I'd explained that she was going to run the agency while I tried to find my brother, she was crying.

I grabbed a box of Kleenex from her desk and dropped it in her lap.

'Dammit, Dana, don't go to pieces on me. I need you to be strong.'

'I am s-strong,' she dabbed at her eyes.

'It's just that . . . '

'I know. You weren't expecting it. Well, join the club.' I went to the coffeemaker and poured myself and Dana a cup, black.

'You don't drink coffee,' she reminded me as I handed her a cup.

'From now on,' I said grimly, 'I'm going to be doing a lot of things I never did before.'

That upset her even more. 'Oh God, boss, I'm gonna miss you so freaking much . . . ' Rising, she hugged me. I hugged her back and together we stood there like a couple of sob sisters, bawling our stupid eyes out.

8

Even before my brother witnessed Kazlov gun down rival mobster Vinnie Bianchi outside Tormentare, an Italian eatery on 7th Avenue, he'd always tried to keep his whereabouts a secret. 'No Known Address' became Danny's standard answer when anyone asked him where he lived. But in fact for a long time before he went into hiding, he lived with and sponged off a very tall, light-skinned black former model from Ipanema called Yolanda in the loft of a converted warehouse in Central Harlem.

I'd known her a while back during her brief stint as a fashion model, and always liked her. She was brassy and out-spoken, but honest, and had genuinely tried to help my brother kick his cocaine habit. Now, as she sat in a pink cushion-chair beside the window overlooking the street, smoking as she watched me rummaging through Danny's things, I couldn't decide if she had told me the truth when she said she had no idea where he was hiding.

'Do you know if he has a P.O. box?' I asked.

'Uh-uh.'

'Would he have told you if he had?'

'Sho like to think so.'

I closed the cupboard where his clothes hung. 'Is he clean, Yolanda?'

'Was when he hit the bricks.' She lit a fresh cigarette from the tip of the old one and sucked in smoke until her cheeks caved. ''Course, I ain't seen him for over a week.'

'You saw Danny a week ago?'

'Month, I meanin' to say.' She nervously licked her big lips. 'Maybe longer.'

'Uh-huh.' Sensing she knew more than she was admitting, I dug through a duffle-bag containing dirty socks and underwear and found nothing I could call a clue. About to give up, I noticed a gold-painted trash can beside a computer desk. It was empty save for some used Kleenex and a tiny crumpled slip of paper on which was written: DD 64097417. Holding it up to Yolanda, I said: 'Any idea what this is?'

She peered through exhaled smoke at the numbers. 'Uh-uh.'

'Then it's not yours?'

'Uh-uh.'

I looked at the numbers again. 'Safety deposit box, maybe? Or an offshore account?'

She shrugged her gorgeous coffee-colored shoulders. 'You'd know better'n me, sister.'

'Too many numbers for a phone number,' I said, adding: 'Mind if I take it with me?'

'Help yo'self.'

I tucked the slip of paper in my jeans and gazed about me. I sensed I'd struck out and couldn't help feeling disappointed. 'If you were looking for him, Yolanda, where would you start?'

'Me, sister?'

'You know him as well as anyone.'

She blew a smoke ring and poked her black-nailed finger through the center. 'Ipanema.'

'Your folks' house, you mean?'

'My folks is dead long time,' she said sadly.

'Then why would Danny go there?'

'Plenty safe place to hide.'

'Plenty of safe places to hide here, too,' I reminded her.

'Not so plenty,' she replied. 'Not if the Man comes a-callin'.' She made a gun with her hand and pressed her forefinger to her head.

'Kazlov's men?'

She nodded and I saw fear in her large black eyes. 'You go now, sister. An' no come back, okay?'

Outside, I got in my Porsche and looked up at the loft. Yolanda was looking out the window. I waved but she didn't wave back. I got the keys out, tucked the slip of paper in my purse, fired the engine and drove off.

9

Twenty minutes later I pulled up outside my building. Lionel Coles, our doorman, stood by the front door talking to one of the tenants. Big enough to block out the sun, he'd been a promising rookie linebacker for the New York Giants a few years back, but eventually got cut when he blew out his knee. He went into freefall after that and according to Kirk, who owned a luxury box at Giant Stadium, was arrested several times for possession and assault. But six months ago he'd finally cleaned up his act and two months ago on Kirk's recommendation I hired him as our doorman. That was the same day — no, the day after my brother was shot at outside the courthouse and then disappeared without telling me. But already in those few weeks Lionel had endeared himself to all of the tenants and I'd learned to trust him — and his street smarts.

As soon as he saw me, he came over, all eyes and teeth. ''Mornin', Miz O' — help you with somethin'?'

'Maybe. Take a look at this.' I showed him the slip of paper. 'Those numbers make any sense to you?'

'Where you get this?' When I told him, he shrugged his massive shoulders and gnawed at his lip. 'I don't do drugs no more, Miz O'.'

'I know that,' I said, adding: 'What's makes you think the numbers are connected to drugs?'

He frowned, concerned. 'Forget it, Miz O'. You don't want no part of this. It bad jive.'

''Meaning?'

'DD, it street for drug dealer. The numbers, they most likely a dealer or a junkie's cell in Harlem.'

'That's too many numbers for a phone number.'

He shook his head. 'The 6 — I'm thinkin' it be short for 646, area code.'

I hadn't thought of that. I handed Lionel my Blackberry. 'Will you call the number for me? See who answers? Please,' I said as he hesitated. 'It's important.'

He sighed and returned my Blackberry, 'Safer I use mine,' took out his cell and punched in the number.

Appreciating the fact that he was trying to protect me, I sat there tapping the steering wheel with my nails, listening to Lionel's conversation.

It was brief, laced with street profanity, and ended with Lionel saying: 'Have a nice day.' Then, chuckling, he tucked his cell away and grinned at me. 'Some ho's don't got no sense of humor.'

'She mention anything about where she was living?'

'Uh-uh. Why?'

'I'm hoping she'll lead me to my brother.'

Lionel frowned, removed his peaked blue cap and rubbed his shaved head. 'I got me a cousin works vice in Central Harlem — I go talk to him, call the number again and he run a check, get you location where this ho's talkin' from, no sweat.'

I studied his large, smooth, impassive face and made a decision.

'How'd you like to spend the day with me?'

He was instantly suspicious. 'Doing what?'

'Whatever it takes to find Danny.'

I could tell the idea appealed to him. 'What about here?'

'The ladies will just have to do without you for one day.' I was smiling as I spoke and Lionel, getting my implication, smiled too. 'I'll pay you whatever you think it's worth.'

'This ain't about money, Miz O'.'

'What, then?'

'Could be you messin' with bad shit here.'

'I'm willing to risk it if it'll lead me to Danny.'

'What if I go check out this crack-head first? Turns out she know your brother, I call you and we all meet someplace?'

'Thanks, but this could be a legitimate lead to Danny and I intend to follow up on it, with or without you. Now, you in or not?'

He grunted, 'Be right back,' and turning hurried into the building.

I looked at the slip of paper and sighed, hoping I knew what I was doing.

10

Despite typically heavy traffic, we made almost every light and it didn't take us long to reach the 32nd Precinct on West 135th Street. Uniformed cops bustled in and out and several blue-and-white squad cars were parked in front of the old-fashioned three-story building. One pulled out just as we drove up and I quickly took its place.

Lionel got out, bent down and spoke to me through the window. 'You sit tight, Miz O'.'

I'm not used to being told what to do, but his hard-eyed expression warned me not to argue. I nodded and watched him enter the precinct. In a tight black T-shirt, jeans, Nike's and no cap covering his glistening shaved head he looked even bigger and more menacing. But he moved with athletic grace and I understood why two of my tenants, hot young divorcees who had money and time to burn, not to mention S-Class Mercedes in the garage, were always finding excuses to have Lionel help them flag down taxis.

I sat there in the Porsche, warmed by the late-Autumn sun, for almost thirty minutes. It could have been boring. But during that time several cute cops came up and smiled at me through the open window. Could they help me with something? No, thanks. Was I waiting for someone? Yes, a friend of mine. Really? What was his name? Maybe they knew him? When I said I didn't think so, since he wasn't a police officer, they weren't deterred. A few asked for my phone number. Under different circumstances I might have been tempted to give out my office number, but today I could only think of finding my brother and after verbally sparring with them I refused, saying that my boyfriend wouldn't appreciate it.

When Lionel finally returned and folded himself into the seat beside me, I could tell by his grin that he had good news.

'Well?' I said eagerly.

'Slam dunk.'

'Don't you mean 'touchdown'?'

'Go, go, Miz O'.'

'Where to?' I asked, starting the engine.

'Central Park, northeast corner. Now, will you go!'

I went.

★ ★ ★

As I drove east toward 5th Avenue, Lionel explained that his cousin had not only pinpointed where the junkie on the phone was calling from — 124th Street and Lenox — but had then gotten on his cell and 'convinced' her that it was in her best interests to cooperate by meeting with us right away. A single mother, hooker and longtime druggie with a criminal record and three kids to feed, she grudgingly agreed to be at Duke Ellington Circle in thirty minutes.

Determined not to be late I drove across Lenox and turned onto 5th Avenue. There was more traffic than I wanted to see. But at least it was rolling. I cut around some slower-moving cars, made a few yellow-red lights and after some fancy maneuvering made it to 110th Street in sixteen minutes. I might have broken the law once or twice — okay, I did break it — but I did not drive any more erratically than every cabbie in the city does on a regular basis — which is why I was surprised when I saw how white-knuckled Lionel was as I parked under some Autumn-clad trees just east of Central Park.

'You all right?' I asked him as we climbed out.

He grunted something I didn't hear, which was probably just as well, and led me across the busy tree-lined street to the little iron-fenced circle — considered the Gateway to Harlem. In the background several luxury high-rise condos stood incongruously near the Lincoln Correction Facility.

Though it was sunny there was a bite to the breeze and red and gold leaves crunched underfoot. We stopped outside the railing by one of the street lights and I looked up at the statue. I'd driven past it on occasion but had never paid much attention to it. I found it impressive. Three black columns, each with three nude Muses atop them, supported the figure of Duke Ellington, who stood beside a concert grand piano. A crowd of mostly young people mingled in the shallow amphitheater. Some were talking in groups, others seated on the steps enjoying the sun or studying.

Lionel nudged me and directed me with his gaze toward the park. A gaunt black woman in a yellow jacket, skin-tight red mini skirt and cheap white-vinyl boots had just come out of Pioneer's Gate and was approaching along the brick sidewalk. She kept close to the railing, constantly looking about her, and when she saw us she stopped, like a frightened deer, and for a moment I thought she might run.

'It's all right,' I told her. 'We're not the police.'

'Easy, girl,' Lionel said as the woman still seemed poised to flee. 'All we wants is information.'

'I don't knows nothin' 'bout nothin',' she said sullenly. 'Wouldn't even be here hadn't been that cop ordered me to.'

'I'm looking for my brother,' I said. I took a snapshot of Danny from my purse and showed it to her. 'Have you seen him recently?'

'Ain't seen him never, lady.'

'Don't you be lying to us, girl,' Lionel warned. 'We got your number from his cell.'

'I'm willing to pay for the truth,' I said. 'Danny needs medicine and will die if he doesn't get it.'

'Maybe I seen him once,' the woman admitted. Her eyes looked haunted, her face ravaged by festering pimples.

'Where?' I asked. 'How long ago?'

The woman extended her palm to me.

Lionel knocked it away. 'After you tell us! And then, only if it's worth something.'

'Please,' I begged her, 'if you know where Danny is, for God's sake tell me. It could mean his life.'

The woman didn't answer. I wanted to grab her and shake the truth out of her. My expression must have said as much because Lionel stretched one huge arm out in front of me, as if to hold me back, while at the same time saying to the woman: 'I make one call, bitch, Welfare come and grab your kids. You be lucky you ever see 'em again.'

All the air went out of her. The anguish in her dark, blood-streaked eyes made me feel sorry for her — till I thought of Danny.

'Yesterday's when I see him last,' she said. 'He make a buy and come by my place to crash.'

'Is he still there?'

She shook her head. 'He don't stay more'n one night no place, lady. 'Fraid of gettin' smoked. He gone already when I get home this mornin'.'

'Where'd he go, do you know?' When she hesitated, I took a hundred dollar bill from my wallet and held it up. 'Tell me and this is yours.'

Eyes fixed on the bill, she said: 'I don't knows where he be for sure, but sometimes he hang out with some chick 'cross from the Apollo.'

'The old theater?'

She nodded.

'We need an address,' Lionel said.

'Don't know no address,' the woman said. She was starting to shake. 'Just knows it's above a shoe store.'

'We'll find it,' I said to Lionel.

He gripped the woman by the arm hard enough to make her wince. 'If you lying, girl, I'll be coming after you.'

'I ain't lyin',' she said. 'I ain't sayin' your brother's there neither,' she said to me. 'Just knows that's where he hang out sometimes.'

'Fair enough.' I nodded to Lionel and he let her go. 'Here,' I gave her the money. She quickly stuffed it into her pocket, looked around as if expecting to be arrested, then turned and hurried back toward the park.

'Let's go,' I told Lionel.

11

'What's your guess?' I said as we drove up 7th Avenue toward West 125th Street — also known as Dr. Martin Luther King Boulevard. 'Think she was leveling with us?'

'Can't never tell about junkies . . . ' Lionel shifted uncomfortably, trying to fit his big body and long legs into the small passenger seat. 'But I wouldn't be getting my hopes up, if I was you, Miz O'. Ain't one of 'em wouldn't sell their soul for a snort.'

He shifted again, this time bringing the knee nearest me up. That's when I caught a glimpse of it. 'My God, Lionel, what the hell you doing with that?' I indicated the ankle holster peeking out the bottom of his jeans.

'Don't hurt nothing to be prepared, Miz O'.'

'And of course you've got a permit for it?'

He just rolled his eyes at me.

'What about when you're working — you carry it with you then?'

''Mean to fight off 312 and 421?'

He was referring to the two divorcees that were hot for him and despite everything, I had to laugh.

'Listen, do me a favor and from now on keep it at home, all right?'

'I can do that.' He grinned, showing capped teeth almost as white as Holly's. 'But you gotta promise to rescue me next time one of them ladies insists I carry her Bloomie's shit up to her condo.'

Now it was my turn to roll my eyes.

* * *

The Apollo Theater isn't the mecca for black entertainers that it was back in the 30's, 40's and 50's — when Ella Fitzgerald, Billie Holliday, Diana Ross, Lionel Hampton and countless others got their start in weekly talent shows. But thanks to the city proclaiming it a Historical Place, thereby protecting it from the wrecking ball, and a massive

56

refurbishing project it's still there, at 253 125th Street, its familiar yellow and red sign jutting out over the neon marquee, offering concerts, performing arts and outreach programs.

Today, when I pulled into a space a few stores past it, the marquee welcomed everyone to 'Amateur Night, Wednesdays, 7:30 PM.' I was too busy worrying about Danny to give it a second glance. Climbing out I joined Lionel on the sidewalk and together we looked at the stores across the busy boulevard.

American Apparel — The Children's Place — Gold City of Harlem — Beauty Land, Luxury Human Hair — High Energy Boutique — Touro College of Pharmacy — Pay Half — the names meant nothing to me, but the fact that not one of the stores had apartments above them did!

'Guess you were right,' I said, disappointed. 'Our junkie friend was blowing smoke.'

'Them that live in hope, die in failure,' Lionel said.

'Charming,' I said irritably. 'If you have

anymore doom and gloom sayings do me a favor and keep them to your — ' I was in the process of turning around as I spoke and broke off abruptly as I saw a sign above the store two doors down from the theater — Orva Shoes! Next to that was a store called Porta Bella that was a combination men's wear and shoe store.

I gripped Lionel's muscled arm and turned him toward the stores. 'Humor me for a minute, okay?'

Then as he patiently listened:

'In her befuddled mind, do you think the woman could've meant next to rather than across from the Apollo?'

He looked at the shoe store and then raised his eyes to the three rows of grimy windows that spanned the building above them. Several cheap banner-type signs hung over the lower windows — Cinderella's Eyebrows Spa — Offices To Let — Cinderella Nails — Office Space — Stores for Rent.

He shrugged. 'Don't say nothing about no apartments.'

'Maybe not. But look up there and there,' I pointed at two rusty window air-conditioners and then at a planter sitting in an open window. 'Couldn't they be apartments — or at least be used as apartments?'

'Come to think of it,' Lionel said, thinking aloud, 'she never say nothing about apartments. Just say your brother hung out with some chick there. Right?'

'Exactly.' I was already walking toward a door that led upstairs.

'Whoa,' he caught up with me and blocked my path in much the same way he'd blocked opposing running backs from crossing the goal line. 'Hold on, Miz O'. Can't be going up there without no game plan.'

'Okay, but make it quick.'

'I go up there first and check things out. Maybe talk to one or two of the tenants — see if they ain't seen a white boy up there recently.'

I looked about me. The people driving past us or walking along the sidewalk in either direction were almost all black and if not black certainly not whiter than a damn statue with green eyes and red-gold hair that reached to my shoulders. 'No way I'm staying here,' I assured him. 'But I will make a concession and let you do all the talking.'

Lionel rolled his eyes. But he decided against arguing and turning, he entered the building. I followed him. The air was stale and smelled like dead cigars. There probably was an elevator but Lionel chose not to use it, instead bounding up the dusty, narrow stairs. I'm fit but it was hard keeping up with him. He stopped at the top of the stairs and while waiting for me to catch up, bent down and removed the gun from his ankle-holster. Pretending not to notice, I looked down the hall and saw it was lined with doors. Most were closed and had faded lettering on them. Halfway down the dimly-lit hall a door was ajar and I could hear women chattering inside.

Lionel tucked the automatic into his pants and covered it with his T-shirt. He then approached the first door and gently tried the handle: it was locked. He put his ear against the door and listened. Then he shook his head at me and moved to the next door. It too was locked and while he listened to see if anyone was inside, I moved to the next door, the one that was partly open and peeked through the crack: several black women were getting their nails painted.

A hand gripped my shoulder and spun me around. Startled, I looked up and saw anger in Lionel's dark, normally-passive eyes. 'Miz O',' he said quietly. 'You my boss and I respect you, but this ain't Park Avenue, it's Harlem, and next time you wander off by yo'self, you on your own. Clear?'

As I said before, I don't like being told what to do. But I also knew if I was to find my brother I needed Lionel, so I nodded. We moved to the last door at the end of the hall. Lionel tried the handle and the door opened inward. An old black man in a shiny black suit with white curly hair lay asleep on an old couch. A desk, two-hard-backed chairs and a gray metal filing cabinet were his only companions. His mouth was open and he was snoring softly. A fly buzzed against the dirty window. Lionel and I swapped glances, decided not to wake the old man and withdrew.

I pointed upward, indicating we should try the next floor. Lionel nodded, quietly closed the door and we headed back to the stairs. I heard Lionel's cell buzz in his pocket. He dug it out of his jeans and checked the caller ID.

'312 or 421?' I deadpanned.

He grinned but didn't answer. I thought I saw a flicker of uneasiness in his eyes. I wanted to ask him if anything was wrong but decided against it. After all, I was his boss not his girlfriend or wife. We started up the second flight of stairs. They creaked underfoot. Lionel stopped and motioned for me to wait. He then, very slowly, climbed upstairs, eyes fixed on the stair ahead. He didn't find whatever he was looking for and pausing at the top, motioned for me to come ahead.

'Sometime a person not wanting to be caught,' he whispered, 'he put something that make a noise on the stairs so he hear you coming.'

I nodded, thinking of an old film noir movie I'd seen on late-night TV in which the framed hero did exactly that; he also wedged a toothpick between the door and the jamb around it so that he'd know if anyone had entered while he was out. While watching the movie I'd never in my wildest dreams thought I'd ever be part of a similar situation.

The next floor had only two tenants. Both were young black men who sat with their feet propped up on old wooden desks, cell-phone in hand, looking uneasy to see us. Neither asked if we were cops, but I sensed they thought we were and their answers were guarded and mildly hostile. I was glad Lionel was with me. Both men confirmed that the other offices were vacant and that only the real estate agent had the keys. Both were equally adamant that no white boy was hanging out in any of them; but the older of the two, a big fleshy man in a black leather jacket and jeans, his head shaved liked Lionel's and his chin sporting a wispy goatee, said he'd seen a white boy climbing the fence that was strung across the vacant lot next to the theater.

'This him?' I asked, showing him Danny's photo.

63

'Could be,' he admitted.

I held the photo closer to him. 'Please try to remember. It's very important.'

He looked again and then shrugged. 'Maybe. I dunno. It was dark an' he wearin' a hoodie. But he 'bout the same age.'

'How long ago was this, brother?' Lionel said.

'Night 'fore last.'

'Any idea where he was going?' I asked.

'Uh-uh. But he in a hurry like he bein' chased.'

I tucked the photo away. 'Thanks for your help.'

The man nodded. I started to dig in my purse for a business card but something in Lionel's eyes told me not to. I turned to leave.

'Be right out,' he told me. I hesitated, saw his tight-lipped expression and left without a word.

In the hall I heard Lionel and the man talking, but couldn't make out what they were saying. Then silence. Then it was just Lionel talking, even more softly. Moments later he joined me and closed

64

the door behind him.

'What was that about?' I said.

'I ask him if any whores turning tricks upstairs.'

'You think the girl Danny was with was a whore?'

'Seemed like a good idea at the time.'

'I'm sorry. I didn't mean to sound judgmental.' I sighed and looked away.

'You ain't gonna cry, are you?'

I turned back to him. 'Not a chance. But next time I act like an ass, you have my permission to spank me.'

Lionel grinned, teeth bright white in the dim hallway. '312, she already got dibs on that.' He had squeezed past me and was starting up the stairs before I could think of a snappy comeback.

12

It was Lionel's idea to remain by the stairs while I knocked on each door. That way, he explained, if Danny was holed up in one of the offices and made a run for it, he, Lionel, could still grab my brother.

It was not only a good suggestion it pushed me to think out of the box. Motioning for him to stay put, I got out my Blackberry and called Yolanda. She answered on the second ring. 'It's Jackie,' I said softly but urgently. 'I've just heard Danny's hiding out with some chick in one of the offices in the building next to the Apollo Theater. I don't know which one but I do know the police are about to show up. Maybe Giacomo's men too, for all I know. Call my brother right away, will you, and tell him to get out of there — fast!' I ended the call before she could argue.

Lionel, who had heard my conversation, arched his eyebrows in approval.

I shrugged. 'Could be a waste of time. But if she is in contact with Danny, like I think, we'll soon know which office he's — '

The door of the second office from the stairs was suddenly yanked open and my brother burst out. He was in an old NYU sweatshirt, jeans and tennies and in the act of pulling on a denim jacket. He saw us and tried to stop, but his momentum carried him forward two more steps — right into Lionel's lunging, out-stretched arms.

Danny fought to break loose, kicking, trying to butt Lionel in the face and calling me every foul name he could think of, but it was useless. Though taller than me and about one hundred and fifty pounds, he was helpless in Lionel's powerful grip.

'Calm down, dammit,' I told him. 'No one's going to hurt you.'

'Not 'less you keep on kicking me,' Lionel growled.

'Then let me go, you sonofabitch!' Danny yelled. His voice was unusually shrill and I could tell by his eyes he was high on something.

Lionel looked at me. I shook my head and he kept his massive arms wrapped around Danny.

'Promise me you won't try to run,' I said to my brother.

'Up yours!'

'Want me to put him to sleep?' Lionel asked me. He quickly changed holds, now gripping Danny in a wrestler's choke-hold, and slowly exerted pressure. 'Now you gonna be quiet, boy? Or do I snap you like a twig?'

Danny, barely able to speak, gasped: 'O-kayyy.'

I nodded at Lionel. He let my brother drop, so suddenly he collapsed to the floor. I kneeled beside him and cupped my hand under his head. 'You okay, Danny?'

He coughed, wheezing and gasping for air, then knocked my hand aside. 'G-Get the hell away from me!'

Surprised by his venom, I straightened up. 'Please, Danny, you've got to listen to me. I have something very important to tell you.'

'Yeah, like give me back my goddamn money!'

'Forget the money,' I said angrily. 'If you needed it badly enough to steal it from me, your own sister, then keep it.'

I could see by the distrust in his glazed blue eyes that he didn't believe me. I could also see that he was very frightened and I wondered if he'd been shot at again. 'C'mon,' I said, helping him sit up, 'let's not argue anymore. Let's go somewhere we can talk — '

Again he knocked my hand away. Then clearing his throat, he glared at me and said: 'Go ahead. Go on, damn you. Get it over with. Kill me.'

'Kill you? What the hell you talking about?'

'You must really think I'm stupid, sis.'

'That's not true. I don't think you're stupid at all. Now, humor me. Why do you think I want to kill you? You're my brother, for God's sake.'

'Then why'd you bring him along?'

He was referring to Lionel, who seemed as surprised as I was.

'Lionel works for me,' I said. 'He only

came along because I asked him to. It's probably dumb, but I was nervous about coming here alone.'

'That's the truth,' Lionel assured him. 'I'm the doorman at your sister's condo building.'

'Bullshit!'

'It's not bullshit,' I began.

Danny wasn't listening. 'He may have got you fooled, sis, but not me. Bastard was there. That night. I saw him.'

'What night? Saw him where?' I said.

'Outside Tormentare. Just before Vinnie got whacked. He was talking to one of Kazlov's clowns.'

'That's ridiculous!'

'Is it? Then ask the D.A.'s office to show you the video I took. He's on it. See for yourself.' Turning to Lionel, he added: 'Why don't you tell her the truth? Tell her who you really work for.'

Lionel grunted in disgust. 'You crazy, man. I don't work for no mobsters and I ain't never even been to Tormen — whatever you called it.'

'More bullshit.'

Lionel looked at me. 'Better straighten

70

out your brother's brains, Miz O', 'fore I slap him 'longside the head.'

'Danny, listen to me,' I begged. 'You're way off-base about Lionel. He's no killer. He used to play for the Giants before I hired him.'

'Sure, two three years ago. But how about after that — when the CFL turned him down and he couldn't even play Arena Football — what's he been doing since then? Breaking kneecaps for Kazlov, that's what!'

'You believe that, you a fool,' Lionel told him. 'You know what I been doing,' he said to me. 'Mr. Harmon, he tell you. He say how hard I been working to get clean — stay sober. If you hadn't believed him you never would've hired me.'

'That's a fact,' I said, including my brother. 'I'll put up with a lot, but I'm death on drugs.'

Danny didn't say anything. His pupils were dilated and I wondered if he'd heard or understood anything I'd said.

'I didn't ought to have to explain it to you, man,' Lionel told Danny. 'You know how it is times when you amped or

71

baseballing in some crack-head's base house. You ain't no good to anybody. Man like Dmitri Kazlov, he know that too.'

His tone had softened and he sounded genuine. My brother chewed his lip, trying to decide what to believe.

'Danny, for crying out loud,' I said. 'Will you stop being so damned paranoid for a moment and ask yourself why I would want to kill you?'

He didn't have an answer but the drugs had twisted his mind and I could tell he was not only scared, but confused.

'All right,' he said finally. 'Let's say I believe you. What's so friggin' important that you gotta chase all the way down here to tell me?'

I hesitated, wondering how much I should tell him in his present state. 'Lionel,' I said, 'give us a minute alone, okay?'

He nodded, moved to the stairs, sat down and began checking his cell for texts.

I rested my hands on Danny's shoulders and looked into his pale, sunken-eyed face. 'I was at Johns Hopkins yesterday for a series of tests. Seems there's some-thing wrong with my blood — '

He frowned. 'Wrong?'

'Yes. A cancer of the white blood cells — '

'Mean, like leukemia?' He actually sounded worried.

'Uh-huh. Chronic leukemia, they call it — or CML for short.'

'Shit.'

'I know, I know.' I saw he was about to break down and knew I couldn't handle that right now. 'But there's no need to panic. There are pills I can take that will help keep it in check — '

'You mean like remission?'

Again I hesitated. Then deciding that telling him I only had a year or two to live might be too much too soon, I said: 'Exactly. Like remission.'

He looked relieved. 'Awesome! Man, you really had me worried there for a minute, sis — ' He stopped as we both heard heavy footsteps climbing up the stairs. Instantly, he panicked and shot me a look of fear mixed with betrayal.

'Wait,' I began.

But he'd already run to the stairs and was looking over Lionel's head at whoever was coming upstairs. His face went white. Turning to me, he hissed: 'You lying bitch!'

'W-What?'

'You sold me out!' Before I could reply, he charged me. I had no time to get out of his way. His lowered shoulder slammed me against the wall. I felt my head snap backward, felt a sharp pain as it hit the wall and then everything went black.

13

Gunshots brought me around. They seemed to be coming from a long way off. I heard voices. I recognized one of them as Lionel's. It too sounded distant. I opened my eyes. Everything looked blurry. I blinked several times and gradually my vision cleared.

The shooting had stopped. I realized I was slumped down with my back against the wall and suddenly remembered Danny had been the cause of it.

Danny!

Getting up, I ran to the open door of the office that my brother had come charging out of. Through the doorway I could see Lionel and a large, burly man in a dark expensive overcoat standing at the open window. Their backs were to me. Both had their guns drawn and were leaning out, watching whatever was going on below. Then I heard footsteps clanking on metal and slowly another big, hard-faced man appeared on the fire-escape.

'Max and Geno — they grabbed him.'

The other man sighed, relieved. 'Thanks for the tip,' he said to Lionel.

I must have moved, maybe from the shock of realizing that Lionel was one of them, because they all whirled around and looked at me.

'You bastard!' I hissed at Lionel — and ran.

A second later I heard shots. Bullets splintered the door jamb inches from where I'd been standing.

I raced down the stairs, praying that I'd reach the bottom before they could shoot me. It was close. I hit the tiny landing, and hand still clutching the railing swung my body around and used my momentum to pull me toward the next flight of stairs. I didn't waste time looking up but Lionel and the two mobsters must have reached the top of the stairs because more shots were fired. Bullets hit the wall, chipping away the plaster near my head.

Fear made me go faster. I galloped down the stairs, two at a time, and made it to the bottom without more shots being fired. They were coming after me now. I could hear their shouting and the rapid thudding of their footsteps. Trying not to panic, I started down the final flight of stairs. But fast as I went, the pursuing footsteps seemed to go faster. I knew they were catching up to me.

Ahead lay the short hallway that stretched from the bottom of the stairs to the door leading to the street. Unconsciously I counted the last few stairs and then, without pausing, leaped off the last stair and hit the floor running.

Behind and above me the pursuing footsteps were getting louder; closer. But the door was only a few steps away. And my car was parked only a quick sprint on along the curb. Once in the Porsche no one was going to catch me. I'd be safe. Relief flooded through me.

That's when I remembered my brother.

14

Yanking open the door I ran out onto the sidewalk. There were no mobsters waiting for me. Nor was there any sign of my brother. Passersby paused to look at me and then hurried on. They wanted no part of a young white woman who looked panicked or the trouble she might be in, and I didn't blame them.

I could see my Porsche parked a short distance ahead. All I had to do was run to it, jump in and drive off — leaving Danny to Giacomo's men.

The decision was mine and it wasn't hard to make.

I'd like to think I would have made the same choice even if I'd had a full life ahead of me. But, regardless, I went to the covered chain-link fence and peered through a tear in the cloth: in the weed-and-litter-strewn vacant lot two big hard cases — presumably Max and Geno — were strong-arming my brother to a black Escalade with tinted windows that was parked on the adjacent street.

I doubted if there was any way I could save his life, but I knew I had to try. Turning, I faced Lionel and the two mobsters who were closing in on me.

★   ★   ★

A little later, when the three of them were escorting me to the Escalade, I heard sirens approaching. Lionel and the mobsters heard them too. They swapped uneasy looks. One of the mobsters, the man I'd seen toiling up the fire-escape, growled: 'C'mon! Hurry it up!'

He was talking to Lionel and the other mobster who'd shot at me. The mobster pulled open the rear door of the SUV and tried to bundle me inside.

That's when Lionel shot him. He fired point blank at the mobster's back and as he went down, Lionel pushed me to the ground. In almost the same motion he whirled and shot the other mobster.

The mobster staggered back, his expression one of shock and rage. 'Y-You rat sonofabitch!' he gasped.

Lionel shot him again, twice, and the mobster stumbled and fell, dead.

He then shot the mobster at the wheel. The bullet punched through the window, shattered glass flying everywhere. From where I lay I couldn't see if the driver was killed; I just know he didn't fire back.

But the mobster in the back seat did. I could see him through the open rear door. It was the one they called Geno. Holding my brother in a neck-lock, he fired twice.

I heard Lionel grunt as the bullets hit him. He staggered back, but managed to get off a shot himself. I couldn't see if Geno was hit. But he let go of Danny and put three more bullets into Lionel.

Lionel stood there a moment, seemingly frozen, and then he dropped his gun and sat down hard. He didn't make a sound. He sat there amid all the litter, clutching his stomach, his usually-stoic face contorted with pain. He was bleeding badly, his clasped hands red with it, and I knew he was dying.

I felt sick.

The sirens were almost on top of us now.

I saw Danny open the far-side door, jump out and run. Geno turned to shoot him but at that moment several blue-and-white squad cars roared up.

Geno screamed at the driver to: 'Go! Go! Go!'

But the driver didn't respond. I craned my neck. Now through the broken window I could see him slumped, motionless, over the wheel.

The squad cars skidded to a stop, blocking both ends of the street. Officers jumped out, guns drawn and positioned themselves behind the cars.

Overhead I could hear a helicopter descending. I looked up and saw it drop out of the sun. It hovered there in silhouette, the rotor blades going whomp-whomp-whomp, a voice over a bullhorn ordering the mobsters to drop their weapons.

Geno threw his gun out of the SUV and climbed out after it, hands held high.

I crawled over to Lionel.

I'd never seen anyone die. But in that

fleeting moment, I saw death in his bloodshot brown eyes and heard death in his rasping voice as he tried to speak.

The thump-thumping of the helicopter's blades hid his words.

I leaned close and put my ear against his drooling lips. I'm not sure what he said but it sounded like, 'S-Sorry c-couldn't tell you,' and then I felt him slump against me and knew he was dead.

15

I never saw where my brother went. I just know that he had disappeared by the time two police officers gently helped me to my feet and led me away from Lionel's corpse.

They put me in the back of a squad car and politely but firmly insisted I wait there until the paramedics and the medical examiner arrived. Not that I was in any condition to argue. I was trembling and jelly-kneed. It's one thing to watch a shootout on television, another thing entirely to be a part of it as it happened, with real people, not actors, dying all around you — especially people you know and care for, like Lionel. It's nerve-shattering and sickening; and as I sat there, looking out the window at the officers cordoning off the area with yellow tape, paramedics arriving and bagging the corpses, television trucks pulling up, the deafening roar of the helicopter as it landed on the vacant lot, I realized just how fleeting life was.

It can be gone in an instant.

Suddenly two years seemed like forever. And if not forever, certainly enough time to find my brother and straighten things out between us.

In my mind I heard Ringo Starr singing: 'Stop and take time to smell the roses.'

It made me think of my folks, who loved the Beatles, and suddenly I found the strength to pull myself together. My dad loved my mother more than life itself. Yet when she died, he bravely went on with his life, keeping his pain to himself while raising Danny and me with all the love he had left.

I could do no less.

16

Kirk has a habit of showing up when you least expect it.

After the paramedics had made sure I was all right I was handed over to a patient, veteran police officer who began taking my statement. Before I was finished, a second chopper landed on the vacant lot and out bounded my ex-husband. He spoke briefly to the brass hat in charge, who allowed him to duck under the tape and hurry over to us.

'That'll have to keep,' he told the policeman.

The veteran officer knew better than to argue. He glanced at the brass hat, who nodded, then closed his notepad and excused himself.

Kirk helped me out of the squad car and kissed me fondly on the cheek. 'Sorry I couldn't get here sooner, Irish, but I had to make a call to get clearance to land my bird at a crime scene.'

I didn't bother to ask him whom he called. He probably wouldn't have told me anyway. I was just grateful to get out of there. As we boarded the chopper and buckled up, Kirk asked me if I knew where my brother had gone. I said no, that I'd just seen him run off, and then it hit me. 'How'd you know Danny was involved in this?'

'You kidding? It's all over the news. You're famous, Irish!'

Having already seen all the television reporters and their cameramen pressed against the police tape, I didn't doubt him. But that didn't answer my question. 'I didn't say me, I said Danny.'

'Why else would you and an undercover FBI agent be in Harlem being shot at by Giacomo's hoods?'

'Undercover FBI — ?' I was so stunned I couldn't finish.

'Sure. Didn't Lionel tell you?'

'Obviously not. And oh-by-the-way, neither did you,' I said angrily.

Kirk chose that moment to tell the pilot to take off. He then gave me a headset and put one on himself. The rotors roared. I felt the chopper lift off and below, through the window, saw the ground dropping away.

'Well,' I demanded over the headset, 'why didn't you?'

'I wanted to,' Kirk said, 'but Lionel told me not to.'

'So much for having no secrets between us.'

'Sorry. But there are some rules even I have to obey.' Before I could reply, he grumbled: 'Idiot! Now they really will go after him.'

'Bastards already tried to kill him twice. How much more can — '

'I don't mean Giacomo. I'm talking about the FBI, CIA, Interpol and God knows whatever else agency they want to bring in to hunt him down.'

'Why would they all be after Danny? He's done nothing wrong.'

Kirk gave an ugly laugh. 'Skipping out on the D.A.'s office, ignoring a subpoena as a state witness, letting a Russian mobster walk away from a murder, and now getting an FBI agent to be killed — you call that doing nothing wrong?'

'Danny didn't get Lionel killed. He had nothing to do with it. You want to blame someone, blame me. I'm the one who asked him to come with me.'

'He would've asked you, if you hadn't.'

'What're you talking about?'

'That's why he took the job as your doorman — to keep tabs on you.'

'On me? Why?'

Kirk shook his head, frustrated. 'You just don't get it, do you?'

'Get what?'

'Your-dear-sweet-not-so-innocent-brother. He's not just an eyewitness who took a video of a gangland murder, he's . . . '

'What?' I demanded when Kirk didn't finish. 'What is he?'

'A paid snitch — informer — stoolie as they used to call them.'

'I don't believe it. Danny wouldn't stoop so low.'

'He would — and he did. Gladly.'

'Why, for God's sake? If he needed money he knew he could always come to me.'

'Not after ripping you off for a hundred

big ones, he couldn't. And even if he could it wouldn't have mattered. This wasn't about money. It was about staying out of prison. The DEA guys nailed him trying to set up a big buy for the Colombians, involving millions in coke, and then offered him a get-out-of-jail card free if he'd be a snitch for them. Since he was looking at a long stretch upstate, he jumped at it. Been working for them ever since.'

I was too numb to say anything.

I gazed out the window. The gleaming skyscrapers and the concrete canyons separating them flew by beneath us. At any other time it was a sight that even a world-weary New Yorker like me would have found stirring. Today I barely saw it. I was too busy trying to make sense out of everything.

'How about you?' I said suddenly.

'How about me — what?'

'You working undercover for the FBI, too?'

He laughed, genuinely amused. 'You're joking, right?'

'Then how come you know so much

about Lionel and Danny and everything else? And don't give me that 'I'm-a-lawyer-of-sorts'-shit, 'cause I'm not buying it.'

He looked at me with those divine, sexy gray-green eyes and for one moment I thought he was about to come clean. Then his phone buzzed. He checked the caller ID, held up a hand to me, 'I gotta take this, Irish,' then removed my headset and tossed it to the pilot.

Now all I could hear was the uneven, thunderous roar of the rotors. We were flying lower now, between the taller skyscrapers, no doubt heading for a landing pad atop one of the buildings Kirk owned a piece of. Turning, I watched him talking on the phone and sensed I would probably never know for sure what he did or how he made his money or knew so many secrets.

Ah, well, I thought. It was probably better that I didn't know. If I did, who knows what I'd think of him. Maybe I couldn't even love him. Or him, me. And right now I needed someone to love me.

All of a sudden I was deadly tired. My eyelids grew heavy and wouldn't stay open. I closed them, just for a second I thought, and fell asleep.

17

The next morning I stopped in at the hospital gift shop and bought a cute stuffed pink giraffe with an adorable grin that I named Steve.

'It's a girl,' the clerk said. 'Pink. Female. Get it?'

So I renamed it Stephanie and headed for the elevators.

A few minutes later, when I entered the little girl's private room a woman was sitting beside the bed. She had the same fair hair and skin as the sleeping child, and slightly resembled her. By her drab clothing, rural-salon hairstyle and makeup, and brown low-heeled shoes no New Yorker would have worn, I guessed she was from out-of-town. Then I remembered the Minnesota plates on the squashed Toyota Corolla and it all came together: she had to be a relative.

'Hi,' I said offering her my hand, 'you don't know me but I'm the one who pulled her from the car.'

The woman rose, shook my hand and gave me a teary-eyed smile. I liked her instantly. 'Oh, but I do know you,' she said, her accent reminding me of the movie, Fargo. 'I'd know you anywhere. You're Jackie O'.'

I was kind of surprised. 'H-Have we met somewhere?'

'No, no, no,' she said as if embarrassed. 'This is my first trip to New York — well, actually my first trip anywhere out of Minnesota. But I've seen you on television, twice in fact. On those morning talk shows — when you won that Business Woman of the Year award.'

Now I was really surprised. 'Ahh,' I said. 'Yes, the award. Yes, well, thank you. And, uhm, you are . . . ?'

'Oh, forgive me — I'm Emma's aunt, Ruby Deitner.' As if realizing who she was herself, she abruptly lost all sense of happiness and became gravely sad. 'It's so tragic,' she said looking at her niece, whose plainly pretty face was heavily bandaged, ' . . . so senseless and terribly tragic . . . I mean we all know the Lord works in mysterious ways, but why He would allow such a dreadful thing to happen, I . . . I . . . ' She broke off as tears flooded from her eyes.

I'd only intended to stay a few minutes, but we ended up talking for almost an hour. The only really important thing I learned was that Emma Hansen was an only child and that when she was able to travel, she was going to live with her Aunt Ruby and Uncle Drew in Park Rapids.

As I was leaving I gave Ruby my card, saying: 'If there's ever anything I can do for her, please don't hesitate to call me or email me and I'll do my best to help.'

'No, no,' Ruby said, 'you've already done too much.'

'I didn't do anything that anyone else wouldn't have done under the circumstances,' I said. 'I just happened to get there first.'

'I don't mean that,' she said, 'though good heavens that's far more than enough. I meant the hospital. Her parents had some insurance of course, and then there's life insurance, though it turns out that that's quite small — '

'Wait a minute, you've lost me. What about the hospital?'

'The bill, the charges for the surgery, doctors and this private room — my goodness, even in Minnesota they'd be outrageous; here, they must be simply astronomical.'

I was beginning to get it. 'You saying everything's paid for?'

'Everything. But you must know that. You paid the hospital.'

'I did?'

'Y-Yes. Didn't you? I mean,' Ruby looked confused, 'if you didn't, who did?'

'Good question.' A name popped into my head and I mentally kissed him. 'Well, don't worry about it. Whoever it was, I'm sure he can afford it.' I gave her a hug and left before things got any more confusing.

Downstairs in the busy lobby I paused and speed-dialed Kirk. 'Nice going,' I said when he came on the line.

'Hello to you too,' he chuckled. 'What's up?'

'Nothing.'

'Then why'd you call?'

'I just wanted to speak to an angel.'

'A what?'

'An angel. You know: someone who drops a miracle on you and then flies off without taking any credit.'

'You must be drunk,' Kirk said, sounding pleased with himself. 'Either that or losing your marbles.'

'No,' I said. 'Neither as a matter of fact. But I am discovering that this world isn't made up only of guys in Black Hats. Now and then a White Hat rides in and saves the day.'

'Care to repeat that over lunch, Irish?'

'Sorry. I can't. I have to pick up my new pills and then catch a flight to Ipanema.'

'Where?'

'You heard me. Ipanema.'

There was a long pause.

'What makes you think Danny's there?'

I laughed. 'As if you don't already know. Hell, you've probably got me tailed twenty-four seven.'

'I wouldn't believe everything Yolanda tells you,' Kirk said darkly.

'This isn't about believing Yolanda or anyone else,' I said. 'It's about clues. And right now this is the only clue I've got and I'm following it.'

'And if he isn't there?'

'I don't know how many countries there are in this world,' I said, 'but until I run out of them, I'll keep looking.' I ended the call and went outside to flag down a taxi.

Part Two

1

A teenage dream of mine, childish as it may seem, was to one day strut my stuff down to Copacabana Beach as the Girl from Ipanema did in the mid-sixties. I'd be just as tall and tanned, just as ogled and aloof to all the wolf whistles and admiring stares as she was on those hot, sunny days when Antonio Carlos Joabim and Vinicius de Moraes sat there, watching her, fascinated, while composing the famous song.

Well, here I am, tall, tanned and in my 'dental-floss' bikini, cruising the sun-drenched beach at Ipanema, getting my fair shares of stares, but nobody's composing songs about me — which, though not great for my ego, is better for someone whose sole reason for being here is to track down her kid brother, Danny, and let him know that I only have a short time to live.

I last saw my brother in Harlem about

a week ago. He was hiding there from the Russian Mafia who wanted to kill him before he could testify as an eyewitness for the D.A.'s office at an upcoming trial in which they hoped to convict the mob boss, Dmitri Kazlov, for murder. I helped Danny elude the mobsters, incurring their anger, and as a result I'm on their hit list too. On top of that Interpol, as a courtesy to the State Attorney, agreed to find my brother and return him to New York City in time for the trial. As you can see, it hasn't been a good year all around!

Why do I think Danny's here, hiding out in Ipanema? Because when I asked his former girlfriend, a gorgeous mulatto ex-model named Yolanda who was born here, where she thought he might be hiding, she replied that if she were looking for him she'd start in Ipanema. Curious, I asked why. She shrugged her lovely coffee-cream shoulders and said because in her home town there were many safe places to hide — places where not even the Russian Mafia would be able to find him.

It made sense, especially since I'd

heard that she and Danny were still a hot ticket, so I left my advertizing agency in the hands of my best friend and business partner, Dana Sheridan, hopped a Varig flight to Rio and paid an airport taxi driver to bring me here. Now, four days later, despite showing Danny's picture around and offering a reward to anyone who could lead me to him, I'm no closer to finding him than I was when I left Manhattan. Worse, I may have tipped him off that I'm looking for him and chased him even farther away.

Why would he run away from me, his own sister who raised him ever since our folks died? Because, through no fault of mine, the mobsters caught up with him in Harlem at the same time I did, leading Danny to believe I'd set him up as payback for hacking into my bank account and stealing a hundred thousand dollars. That's why I'm anxious to find him quickly — I can't go to my grave knowing my brother thinks I'm capable of having him killed!

Deep in thought, I tripped over the tanned, muscled leg of a sunbather stretched out on the sand in front of me.

'Oh, hey — I'm sorry,' I said, managing to remain upright. 'You all right?'

The muscular man I'd stepped on got up, taller than me by several inches, and flashed a smile that was hard to resist. 'You are American, yes?' he said in accented but flawless English.

'Uh-huh.'

'And you are here, in my country, to enjoy yourself?'

'That's probably on the agenda somewhere.'

'Then I will forgive you, bella senhora, on one condition.'

'I have lunch with you, right?'

He flashed those white teeth again. 'You make it sound like a prison sentence.'

I sighed and shifted my feet on the hot sand. 'Look, Fernando,' I said wearily, 'I don't mean to be rude, but I've spent the last few days traipsing around from here to Sugarloaf and right now I'm tired and irritable — '

'Argentinian,' he said, interrupting.

''Scuse me?'

'Fernando Lamas, the famous MGM movie star — he was Argentinian, not Brazilian.'

'Oh-h . . . well, I'm sorry. But I don't go back that far. I was referring to his son, Fernando Lamas junior. And I think he's American.'

'You mean Lorenzo, not Fernando.'

He was right, of course, and I laughed to hide my embarrassment.

'If you are willing to have lunch with me, bella senhora, I will change my name to Lorenzo or Fernando or anything else to please you.'

He and the muggy heat were wearing me down. 'Okay, okay. But I also have a condition — quit calling me beautiful lady. It's corny and makes me think I'm being hit on by a gigolo.'

'As you wish,' he said graciously; and the clown actually bowed.

★   ★   ★

We ate lunch across the street at the glassed-in patio-restaurant of the Ipanema Hotel. The hotel staff referred to it as a porch, which sounded somewhat unromantic, but the food there was great and the views of Rio's coastline nothing short of stunning. But it wasn't the food or the view that made me decide on this particular restaurant: I just felt safer lunching with a hunky beach-lizard in the hotel where I was staying.

Fernando's real name, he said, was Juan-Carlos Albanez. When I asked him what he did for a living, he replied that he was a former polo player who'd had to retire early due to a bad leg injury. I didn't argue with him — since it didn't matter to me anyway — but I was a little suspicious about where the scars were since the multicolored Brazilian-cut speedo he was squeezed into was half the size of my bikini bottom. But Rio de Janeiro wasn't called 'Flesh City' for nothing, so I just smiled, nodded and ate my lobster salad and drank my cerveja from a frosty glass.

Finally he said something that caught my attention. 'What would it be worth to you if I found your brother?'

'How do you know I'm looking for my brother?'

'I have ears and I listen when the streets talk to me.'

'In other words, it's all over town?'

'Did you expect it not to be? Let me rephrase that,' he added before I could reply. 'Wasn't that your goal? If it weren't, surely you would not have shown his picture around or offered a reward for information leading to — '

'All right, all right, you've made your point.' I held my Bohemia up and signaled to the waiter for another. 'I'll pay you the same amount I'd pay anyone who can lead me to Danny.'

'Double.'

'Double?'

'Double. And make up your mind quickly, aka: Jackie O', or the next time you ask me it will be triple.'

I stared at him, unable to believe his gall. 'I didn't 'ask' you the first time, amigo, so don't be putting words into my mouth. And as for paying you double, how about giving me one good reason I should pay you at all?'

'Because if your brother is here, I will find him. That is a promise.' He rose, bowed, flashed his smile and stalked out.

I watched him cross the Avenue Vieira Souto that runs alongside the ocean and join a bunch of tanned hunks peacocking on the sand.

I disliked and distrusted his type but for some unfathomable reason I believed in him.

2

After I'd finished my beer I took the elevator up to the 6th-floor ocean-front suite I'd rented and called my ex-husband, Kirk Harmon, in Manhattan.

Though divorced, we still cared for each other; and, despite our often-heated differences, were always willing to help one another out. It galled me that I still relied upon Kirk occasionally, but I have to admit his strength was comforting during times of duress. Kirk, bless him, made it easier on me by never reminding me that I was using him or his wealth and influence, and day or night was always there for me — even when it included helping me to find my brother whom he disliked and felt I'd be better off without.

'Hi, it's me,' I said when he answered his private phone.

'Hey, Irish — listen, can I call you back in thirty minutes. I'm in the middle of something here.'

'Sure. Oh, and give her a double-dip for me.' I hung up. As I did I remembered that Rio was in a different time zone than New York and wondered what time it was there. I called the front desk and was told by the operator that New York was three hours behind Rio. I checked my satellite phone and saw it was a few minutes before one. I did the math. What the hell was Kirk doing in bed with a woman at ten in the morning? Even shady billionaires, who claim to be 'a lawyer of sorts,' had schedules and appointments to keep. Before I could figure it out, the bedside phone rang.

'That was quick, Don Juan. Wasn't she your type?'

I expected a chuckle. Instead a deep, Brazilian-accented voice told me stiffly: 'Excuse me, this is the manager, Senhora O'Hara. I just wondered if you needed anything else?'

'Uh-hm, no thanks. I'm good. But thanks for checking anyway — ' He'd already hung up. So much for witty repartee!

'Who is this?' I growled when my cell finally buzzed.

'Cute,' Kirk said. He was irked and I guessed I was responsible. 'Now, what's your problem?'

'Hey,' I said, flaring, 'don't get pissy with me 'cause one of your hump sessions didn't work out.'

'Jesus,' he breathed. I could almost hear him counting to ten. 'Is this what I get for interrupting my call to the President of the Bank of Zurich — my balls handed to me!'

He sounded seriously pissed and immediately I felt bad. 'Look, I'm sorry I yelled at you — okay? Ok-kay?' I added when he didn't reply.

'Just tell me what you want, Irish.'

'I met a guy — probably a local gigolo — who says he can find Danny. His name's Juan-Carlos Albanez — ' least, so he says.'

'And you want me to check him out — see who he really is?'

'Clairvoyancy,' I said, 'is a wonderful thing.' I ended the call before Kirk got really sore and took a cold shower. I was just finishing drying off when I heard my cell buzz. I ran to the bed and picked it up. 'Talk to me.'

'He's a former polo player who got permanently kicked off the world circuit for shaving points.'

Surprised that Juan-Carlos had ever played polo, I said: 'That's it?'

'That's it.'

'No wife, ex-wife or girlfriend or family or anything?'

'Not on record.'

'How about his past, like where he was born, grew up, blah, blah?'

'Nada.'

'Hm-mm . . . ' I thought a moment. 'So should I trust him or not?'

'Never trust anyone, Irish. Haven't you learned that by now?'

'That include you?'

'Me most of all,' he said. But he was chuckling as he said it and before I could find a suitable retort, the line went dead.

3

By early evening it had cooled down a little and while it was still light I went jogging in the square that was three blocks behind the hotel. I would have preferred to run on the beach but the hotel concierge said that Praca Nossa Senhora da Paz was better-lighted and therefore safer.

I do some of my best thinking while I'm jogging but this was not one of those 'Eureka moments!' as Dana calls them: the only decisions I made were that I would eat dinner at the hotel tonight, go to bed early to get extra shut-eye, then in the morning sunbathe on the beach and hope that Juan-Carlos contacted me. Without slowing down, I made one more circuit of the square and started back to the hotel.

Waiting in the lobby for me was Juan-Carlos. He was in tight white jeans and a royal blue shirt open almost to his waist. His black hair was slicked straight back and gleamed under the lobby lighting. I hated to admit it but when he smiled and waved to me, my blood pressure soared. He was that hot. Forcing myself to be calm, I went over to him. 'Please, whatever you do,' I said as he got up, 'don't bow.'

He looked hurt. His big dark eyes, almost hidden beneath long lashes any woman would die for, studied me intently as if searching for some kind of weakness he could use to his advantage. Finding none, he said: 'As you wish, senhora. Though I must tell you, most women — especially American women — are enchanted by my bowing.'

'I'll make up for it by buying you a drink,' I said and led the way to the bar. Inside, it was crowded and noisy and the air-conditioning was struggling to keep it cool. We managed to grab two stools at the far end of the bar and knowing how macho Brazilian men are I let Juan-Carlos order the drinks. If he noticed my noble gesture he never showed it — just as he never attempted to pay for the check. Ah well, I've always said there was no such thing as a free lunch.

We sat there talking, each drinking a caipirinha, a potent drink made from cane sugar rum, lime juice and sugar, and though I didn't mention it I kept expecting him to explain why he was waiting for me in the lobby. He didn't. We finished our drinks and without asking me he ordered two more caiprinhas, waited for me to pay for them then picked them up and told me to follow him. Since he was already on the move, squeezing between the groups of attractive, brash, mostly-young customers toward the exit, I had little choice but to tip the bartender and follow him.

Outside, he stood waiting for me on the white-and-black patterned sidewalk that stretched for miles, all the way to Copacabana and beyond.

'Listen, before we go any farther,' I said, 'what's this all about? Were you waiting for me just to bum a few drinks or do you have something important to tell me?'

Juan-Carlos laughed. 'Americans, you

are all so impatient. Why can you not take time to smell the lilacs along the way?'

'Probably for the same reason you talk in clichés — and it's 'roses' not 'lilacs'.'

'So you were listening,' he smirked.

I wanted to slap him, but the caiprinha was already mellowing me out. 'Listen,' I said, 'for the last time, what's going on?'

'I thought perhaps you'd be more comfortable drinking these on the beach. It's quieter there and there are no camera-phones or videos recording our meeting.'

'Why would anyone want to record our being together?'

'One never knows,' he said mysteriously. 'This is Rio, after all.'

I had no idea what he meant by that, so I let it go and followed him across the broad avenue to the beach.

'All right,' I said sitting beside him on the cooling sand. 'We're here. Give.'

He answered by handing me both drinks. He then unbuttoned the top of his jeans, revealing he wasn't wearing under-shorts, unzipped about two inches and just as I was about to get up and leave, took a folded business card out of a tiny inner pocket. Taking back his drink, he palmed me the card, saying: 'Do not make it obvious you are reading this.'

All this cloak-and-dagger stuff reminded me of one of those old Peter Sellers-Inspector Clouseau movies and I had a hard time not laughing. Then I read what was printed on the card and my mouth fell open.

'Th-this is a joke, right?'

'Do you see me laughing, senhora?'

'No. But if you're serious, there's something I ought to tell you, amigo. I had a friend of mine in New York check you out and all he could find was that you'd been kicked out of professional polo for shaving points. It didn't say anything about this,' I pointed at the business card, adding: 'By the way, how does one shave points in polo?'

'By deliberately missing a goal when a certain score, previously set by gamblers, is reached.'

'But surely that's obvious to the judges and the crowd?'

'Not if one is clever and makes it appear as if your pony's to blame.'

'You mean 'cause it turned the wrong way or something?'

'Exactly. Polo ponies are trained to obey the slightest touch of the reins or your knees. Every fan knows that. So if during a chukker — '

'A what?'

'Chukker — a period during a match. Like a quarter in American football only in polo there are six chukkers. Anyway,' he continued as he saw I understood, 'if a pony were to suddenly disobey a command and inexplicably turn in the wrong direction, then the rider can hardly be blamed for missing an otherwise simple shot.'

'But why would it if it's so well-trained?'

He smiled, teeth flashing white against his darkly tanned skin, and said: 'Who's to say that that wasn't part of its training?'

'Hey,' I said, catching on, 'that's pretty nifty. But apparently, in your case, J.C., not nifty enough?'

He shrugged. 'I was ratted out, as you Americans say.'

'How come?'

'I got greedy. Threatened to go public with everything if I didn't get a bigger cut.'

'Ah. So they went public anyway but made you the fall guy?'

'Sadly, yes.'

'Did you go to prison?'

'I would prefer not to discuss that.'

'Fair enough.' I remembered the card I was holding. 'So after you got banned, you went into the private eye business?'

Juan-Carlos nodded, took his card back, folded it and tucked it back into the inner pocket, but did not zip up his jeans.

'Just so we understand each other,' I said darkly, 'I have no interest in you sexually (a lie if there ever was one), so unless you're looking to get busted for flashing me, I'd put that big boy to bed.'

He shrugged, zipped up, gulped some of his drink and gazed out at the darkness gathering above the ocean.

'Why so secretive about being a PI?' I asked.

'I will be honest with you.'

'I can't tell you how thrilled that makes me.'

'Sarcasm doesn't become you, senhora.'

'Then knock off the drama queen act and get to the steak.'

'The two images clash,' he said after a pause. 'So I keep them separate. That way, beautiful women do not fear I am spying on them for their husbands or lovers.'

'Makes sense,' I said. 'But I'm not old enough to need a gigolo yet, so it won't affect me. Now, let's get down to business. How much do you charge?'

'For you — I am free.'

'Thanks, but that's not how it works. I like to pay as I go. That way, I'm not indebted to anyone. So, how much will it cost me?'

'Per hour or per day?'

'Per day.'

He named a figure.

'That's pretty steep.'

'I am the best at what I do.'

'Just ask you, right? Okay,' I said after a pause, 'you've got a deal. But I warn you, my friend — you don't produce, you're out on your ear.'

'Americans,' he said, straight-faced, 'you have such colorful ways of expressing yourselves.'

4

We spent the rest of the night looking for my brother.

Ipanema, unlike most of Rio — which due to increasing poverty, crime and a slumping world economy has lost much of its luster — is a chic, trendy neighborhood that buzzes with fashionable designer boutiques, art galleries, avant-garde theaters, cyber-cafés and a thriving nightlife.

Juan-Carlos seemed well-known everywhere we went. Yet despite his apparent popularity, no one that we showed Danny's photo to had seen him or anyone who even looked like him. Night turned into early morning and still we wandered from club to club, bar to bar, café to café without success. Since I was footing the bill, I wanted to make sure this wasn't a scam by Juan-Carlos to enjoy a free night on the town. He assured me it wasn't. He seemed sincere, or as sincere as someone with his charisma and glib charm could be, and having no real alternative other than to up the reward or fly home, I went along with him.

But by three a.m., I'd had enough. I insisted he flag down a cab, got in and went back to my hotel. There, I yawned my way up to my room, swiped the lock with my card-key and pushed open the door.

Instantly, someone slammed into me, knocking me sprawling into the hall. My head hit the carpeted floor hard enough for lights to explode behind my eyes. I didn't see the masked intruder's face, but I did hear someone running away. Dazed, I lay there a moment, trying to collect myself. As my head slowly cleared, I sat up and looked around. My attacker was gone. So was my purse! Swearing, I ran into my room and called the front desk.

I explained about the robbery to the night clerk, who assured me that no one had passed him in the last few minutes, which meant the thief must have left by the rear exit. Did I need medical attention he added, and should he call security.

I said no to the first question and then asked him to hold while I checked the safe. It was on the floor in the closet. I punched in my password and looked inside. My passport, visa, extra credit cards and money lay there, untouched. Relieved, I returned to the phone and told the clerk that nothing I could think of had been stolen, so there was no need to call security. He apologized for the inconvenience, assured me that nothing like this had ever happened before, said good night and hung up. Moments later there was a knock on my door.

'Yeah, who is it?'

'Hotel Security, senhora.'

'I just told the clerk not to call you.'

'Open up, please.'

I yawned, deadly tired, and said: 'Slide your ID under the door.'

I waited, eyes locked on the bottom of the door, and after a moment an ID card appeared. I checked it, decided it was real and opened the door.

Facing me stood two men. The closest man was dark-skinned, big as a forklift, had a gold front tooth and wore a blue-gray uniform with a nametag and shoulder patches marked: Security — Ipanema Hotel.

The man behind him was — Juan-Carlos Albanez!

'What the fuck,' I began.

'May we come in, senhora?'

I stepped aside, fully awake now, and shot Juan-Carlos a look that by all rights should have withered him. Immune, he merely nodded politely to me and spoke rapidly to the security officer. I don't speak Portuguese, so had no idea what he said, but after a brief look around the officer said good night and left.

Juan-Carlos closed the door behind him and turned to me. 'Are you all right?' he said, genuinely concerned.

I nodded, though the lump on the back of my head throbbed painfully.

'What happened?'

'Tell me why you're here first.'

He studied me, all signs of superficial charisma and gigolo charm gone, his deep-set dark eyes no longer cruising my body or undressing me, and with character lines beside his tight-lipped mouth I hadn't noticed before — in fact, if I hadn't known better, I would have sworn that the Juan-Carlos who had hit on me at the beach and later escorted me around Ipanema and the man standing before me now, were two different men: twins maybe.

'I'm afraid you must be the one to answer first, Ms. O'Hara.' As he spoke he took out his wallet and flashed his ID at me.

'Holy Moses,' I said, shaken. 'Interpol?'

He nodded. 'Now, what happened? And please, do not leave anything out. It may be important.'

'Nothing happened,' I said. 'I got off the elevator, opened the door, this guy came charging out of my room, knocked me on my butt, stole my purse and took off. End of story.'

'You are positive it was a man?'

'Yes. No. I mean I didn't see his face. But if it wasn't a guy, then you're looking for a two-hundred-and-fifty pound woman who's at least six feet and hits like a middle-linebacker. Uhhm, that's a foot-ball player if — '

His chiding look cut me off.

'What was inside your purse — do you remember?'

'The usual stuff. Money, Amex card, lipstick — '

'How about jewelry?'

'Uh-uh. My travel agent warned me about all the grab-and-run robberies going on down here, so I left everything behind.'

His cell buzzed. He excused himself, motioning with one hand for me to stay put, entered the bedroom and closed the door. He returned beside me a few minutes later, looking more concerned than ever.

'What?' I said.

'Your purse — security found it on the stairs by the rear exit. It appears, they say, that nothing of value was taken from it. Your American Express card, driver's license, money, cell phone — all are still inside.'

Relieved, I said: 'A tender-hearted thief, how lucky is that?'

'It would have been better all around,' Juan-Carlos said, not amused, 'if they'd been stolen.'

'Speak for yourself, Charlie. I don't know about you, but for us private jokers getting a new driver's license alone is a big hassle — '

'You don't understand, Ms. O'Hara. The fact that the thief did not steal anything tells me that he was not a thief at all — '

'Then why steal my purse, or be in my room in the first place?'

'Precisely,' Juan-Carlos said.

'Oh-h,' I said as the penny dropped. 'You mean he had some other agenda and — and I can tell by the way you're scowling at me, you think it's got something to do with my brother. Right?'

'Or the Russian Mafia.'

'Those jerks are here in Rio, too?'

'They're everywhere, Ms. O'Hara. Just as drugs are.'

'Drugs? You saying you think I'm here to sell drugs?'

'Not you, no. But the M.O. fits your brother.'

'And he's using my hotel suite as a drop, that your scenario?'

'I have no 'scenario,' Ms. O'Hara. But,

since you brought it up, such a scenario is not out of the question, don't you agree?'

'No, dammit, I don't agree. I'm death on drugs. Everyone who knows me even vaguely knows that. At home I even make donations to various organizations whose goal is to prevent the spread of drugs. So — '

'Be that as it may, Ms. O'Hara, your feelings toward drugs does not extend to your brother. For all you know, he hides drugs here while you're out — '

'How the hell can he do that? He needs a key to get in, unless of course he kicks the door in, which seems unlikely since that would alert not just me but the maids and hotel security — '

'Both of which could be involved — '

'You serious? You think Danny's bribing the hotel staff so he can use my room for a drop or a buy? C'mon now, Juan, that's a stretch even for you, Interpol Agent extraordinaire, wouldn't you agree?'

He flushed, stung by my sarcasm.

'Ms. O'Hara — '

His officious attitude pissed me off.

'Whoa, whoa, hold the bus,' I said. 'Do me a favor, okay? Drop the attitude. Stop being so damn formal all of a sudden. After trying to get in my pants for the past twenty-four hours, it makes you sound ridiculous.'

For a moment he looked insulted. Then he must have realized I was right because he relaxed and said: 'It hasn't quite been twenty-four hours, Jackie. Just seems like it.'

'Amen to that.'

'So how about a truce?' He offered me his hand and smiled — not his gigolo smile or his PI smile but his calm, quiet, darkly handsome Interpol Agent smile that melted my anger and triggered warning alarms inside me.

I ignored them. 'Oh, shit,' I said. Then I did what I had wanted to do ever since he'd walked in the door. I kissed him.

5

After Juan left, I took a quick shower and fell into bed. I was about to drift off when my cell buzzed. Groaning, I sleepily checked the caller ID. I expected it to be Juan, but it was Kirk.

''Lo?'

'Hi. You sound sleepy. Did I call at a bad time?'

'It's three-thirty in the freakin' morning!'

'It is? Oh, hey, I'm sorry, Irish. I counted forward instead of backward — or the other way around, I can't remember. Go back to sleep — '

'Wai-wai-wait! Don't hang up. I'm awake now.' I sat up, yawned so hard it made my jaw ache, and punched the pillows comfortable before settling back against them. 'Talk to me. What's up?'

'Nothing,' Kirk said. 'Just wanted to see how you were doing.'

'Fine. Well, fine except for the fact I

almost got robbed — '

'ROBBED?'

'Take it easy. Nothing happened. This clown knocked me down and grabbed my purse and took off. But I got it back, so — '

'Goddammit! I knew I shouldn't have let you go to Rio alone.'

'First off, you didn't let me, buddy boy, you couldn't have stopped me. And secondly, I just told you — I'm fine. I really am. I haven't dug up any clues as to where Danny is, which sucks, but hopefully that'll change and — oh, by the way,' I added through another yawn, 'did you and the Bank of Zurich ever make up?'

'Bank of — ? Oh-h, my call to the President? — sure, sure, Horst understood. He and I are old friends. He's pretty cool — for a Swiss guy. Dealing with most of them is like shaking hands with an icicle. I remember in one meeting . . . '

I must have fallen asleep because the next thing I remembered was waking up with a start and seeing my cell open in my hand. There was a crack in the blinds and a pole of sunshine striped the bedclothes over my still-raised knees. I held the cell in the light and peered at the face plate screen. A text from Kirk read: 'When you wake up, call me. Love, K.'

I chuckled. Yawning, I lazily stretched. My stomach rumbled and I realized I was starving. I love food and I'm always hungry. If I didn't exercise so much, I'd probably be fat. Well, overweight anyway. But vanity rules and forces me to maintain my figure and stay healthy. I called room service and ordered blueberries, OJ, croissants and decaf coffee. I then got up and did my stretching exercises. I know it sounds stupid to keep fit when you only have a year or two to live but I always try to look on the bright side. I mean, who knows, maybe they'll find a cure for chronic leukemia and I'll beat the odds and live to be a hundred.

Going to the window, I pulled the blind aside and looked out. Traffic raced past in both directions on the avenue and there were already sun-worshippers and joggers on the beach. Kids, burned almost black by the sun, body-surfed in the breaking waves. The shadows of four volleyball players chased their owners on the powdery yellow sand. The ocean had a dark purple tint to it. Seagulls hovered above the white caps, one occasionally swooping down to grab a fish. I was tempted to cancel breakfast and go for a run. But I knew my stomach would never speak to me again, so I wandered into the bathroom and took a shower. By the time I'd toweled off, dried my hair and put makeup on, I heard someone knocking.

I grabbed my robe, went to the door and opened it. I expected to see a waiter. But instead it was Juan-Carlos wearing the waiter's white jacket with a wheeled breakfast cart. 'Good morning, senhora!'

'Go away,' I said. 'It's too early to deal with you — either one of you.'

Ignoring me, he pushed the cart in. Then removing the jacket, he gave it to the real waiter standing behind him and said something in Portuguese.

'What did you tell him?' I asked when the cute young waiter just stood there, grinning at me.

'That, like all Americans, you were a big tipper.'

'Judas.' I rolled my eyes, went to my purse on the table and dug out my wallet. I hadn't fully figured out the currency yet, so I gave Juan-Carlos a wad of bills, expecting him to extract the right amount. Instead he peeled off half the money and handed it to the waiter. The kid gave a huge grin and thanked me profusely, 'Brigadao, brigadao, brigadao!' before hurrying out.

'What'd I do,' I said as Juan-Carlos gave me back the remaining money, 'buy him a new car?'

He shrugged. 'Gabriel's a good boy. No drugs, supports his mother and two sisters — he deserves a break. Besides, you can take it off my bill if you like.'

'You're too generous.' I poured myself some coffee. 'Which reminds me, Mr-Interpol-Agent, why didn't you tell me who you really were right off? Why the dog and pony show about being a gigolo and then a PI? And that fake business card hidden in your jeans — I mean, c'mon, what's that all about?'

Juan-Carlos shrugged, as if to say it was all part of the job.

'That's your best answer?'

'There is a saying in Brazil,' he said: 'Eo jeitinto brasileiro.'

' 'It's the Brazilian way.' Yeah, I've heard of it. So?'

'The same applies to Interpol.' Helping himself to a croissant, he opened the slider to the balcony, went out and plopped down on one of the recliners.

Realizing I wasn't getting anywhere, I took my coffee out on the balcony. He looked surprised that I hadn't brought him coffee too, and I, sucker that I am, handed him my cup and returned inside to pour some more.

'Just tell me one thing,' I said when I rejoined him. 'Are you going to keep switching roles on me? 'Cause if you are, I'd like to know upfront. It's really confusing. Disconcerting, too. Damned disconcerting. I mean one guy makes my flesh crawl and the other, well, he . . . '

'Go on,' Juan-Carlos said. 'What about the other 'guy'?'

'He makes my flesh crawl too. But in a good way.'

'Sexy way?'

'That too.'

'I'll try to remember that.' He sipped his coffee, then set the cup down on the glass-topped table, swung his legs over the side of the recliner and looked at me, concerned.

'Uh-oh, I don't like that look. What's wrong?'

'I believe you're in danger, Jackie. And not just from the Russian Mafia, but someone closer to home.'

'Serious?'

'Deadly serious.'

That knocked the wind out of me.

'Like, who for instance?'

'I don't know — yet.'

'Take a guess. I mean you must know more than you're telling me or you wouldn't have said anything.'

He sipped his coffee as he considered. 'I have a contact — '

'A mole, you mean?'

He continued as if I hadn't spoken. 'This person says that although the

Russians undoubtedly intended to kill you that day in Harlem, they do not consider you enough of a problem to pursue you or put out a long-range hit on you.'

'That's nice to know.'

'Don't misunderstand. That doesn't mean that if you happened to be around if and when they found your brother they wouldn't whack you too — odds are they would. But as of this minute, there is no specific contract out on you.'

'That's a relief.' I absorbed his words before adding: 'If not the Russians, who else could it be?'

'I was hoping you might tell me.'

'Then we're in trouble because I have no idea.'

'Think. Hard. You must've stepped on a few toes over the years.'

'Sure. Who hasn't? But off the top of my head I can't think of anything I've done or any person I might've wronged hating me enough to want me dead.'

'What about your brother?'

'What about him?'

'Does he stand to inherit your business

— any money, stocks, bonds, whatever — if you die?'

'Sure. Everything I have goes to him — wait a minute,' I said as it hit me, 'are you saying Danny's out to kill me so he can get his hands on my money?'

Juan-Carlos shrugged. 'It's possible, isn't it?'

'Anything's possible. But it's also absurd. My brother and I have locked horns a few times over the years, but never anything really serious — nothing more than most siblings go through now and then.'

'In your opinion maybe.'

'Meaning?'

'How about putting yourself in his shoes — thinking like he thinks. Anything jump out at you then?'

I thought of all the falling outs Danny and I'd had since our folks died; the arguments about finishing school, fights over his drug addiction, poor choice in girlfriends, of not being able to hold a job for more than a few weeks — sometimes even days — but I still couldn't pinpoint any particular blow up that I thought would make Danny want to kill me.

'Well?'

I shook my head. 'Nope. Nothing that I deserve to die for.'

' 'Deserve' has nothing to do with dying or living, Jackie. You of all people should know that.'

' 'Of all people' — what's that supposed to mean?'

He looked uncomfortable.

'You know I have CML?' I said, surprised. Then as he nodded: 'Hell, maybe I should hire a skywriter and have him spell it out over the city so everyone in Rio knows!'

'Take it easy.'

'You take it easy!' I was almost shouting. 'You're not the one who has to look in the mirror every morning and know it's all going to end in not much more than a blink of an eye.'

'I'm sorry,' he said. 'I didn't mean to upset you.'

I sighed, grumbled something about it not being his fault, then: 'It's just so damn' frustrating. I mean, except for getting really tired now and then, occasional pains in my hips and bruising easily, I feel like a million bucks. And yet all the time I know it won't be that way for long. Like the doc says: as the disease progresses, becomes more virulent, I'm going to start feeling like shit. But . . . right now . . . ' I broke off, unable to finish, and stared out at the green ocean, my gaze following a sunburned tourist para-sailing behind a rocketing speed-boat.

Juan-Carlos didn't say anything for several minutes. But I could feel him looking at me. He then reached out and pressed his hands over mine. 'If you'll let me be serious for a moment . . . '

'Knock yourself out.'

'Jackie, look at me, please.'

Grudgingly I obeyed.

'For the time being, at least until I can find out who is trying to kill you, I must keep playing gigolo and private detective. It may seem foolish, even annoying, but it is the only way I can stick close to you . . . twenty-four seven.'

I nodded. 'How's that work exactly? Does it include spending nights here, in the suite, or having some cretin standing outside my door all night?'

'Probably some of both.'

'Well, well,' I said. 'Seems either way you get what you want.'

'What's that?'

'Keys to my city.'

I was joking but he didn't find it funny.

'That was a mistake,' he said quietly. 'It won't happen again.'

'Thanks a lot.'

'Surely you understand why it can't.'

I gave an ugly laugh.

'Understand? Ha. I don't understand any part of this crazy charade.'

'I'm sorry.'

'I'm not. Christ, Juan, we're not children. We're adults. And where I live, adults don't stick their hands in the cookie jar and then cry foul.' I got up, angry now, and stormed into the bedroom. I heard his recliner scrape as he got up and followed me.

I timed it perfectly. The slammed door hit him in the face.

6

Fortunately, my temper soon cools off. After a few minutes, I opened the door and entered the living area. Juan-Carlos was sitting on a stool bent over the counter, a towel packed with ice pressed against his nose.

'Oooops,' I said.

He mumbled something into the towel that I didn't hear.

I moved closer to get a better look. That's when I saw blood on the towel. 'Oh, God,' I said. 'I'm sorry. Here, let me help you with that.'

He glared at me over the towel and repeated what he'd said earlier, only this time I heard him.

'Wow,' I said. 'Guess I'm not the only one with a bad temper. Do you want a drink?' I added, going to the bar. 'It's on the house.'

He shook his head.

'Oh,' I said. 'On duty now, are we?'

He removed the towel, revealing a swollen once-bloody nose. 'You're a certified nut case, aka: Jackie O'. It'd serve you right if I walked out and left you to fend for yourself.'

'But you won't,' I said. 'That'd go against your moral code.'

'Don't count on me having morals, period.'

'But I am counting on it. Besides, I said I was sorry. What more do you want? Remember, I'm not the one putting the bedroom off-limits, so I'm not entirely responsible for what happened.' I fixed two Bloody Marys, sans celery sticks, and brought them over to him. 'Here,' I said, setting his on the counter before him. 'Consider this medicinal. It'll help what ails you.'

Reluctantly, he set the towel on the counter and took a sip.

'There, isn't that better?'

He was too stubborn to even nod.

Latinos!

Halfway through our Bloody Marys my cell buzzed. I took it out of my robe pocket, looked at the caller ID then quickly answered the call. 'Yolanda! — hi, this is a nice surprise — what's up, girl?'

The voice that answered sounded panicked. 'I must talk to you, right away!'

'Why? What's wrong?'

'I explain when I see you.'

'That could be a while. I'm in Rio — well, Ipanema actually, looking for Danny.'

'I know that, sister. That is why I call. I am here also.'

'You're in — Ipanema?'

'Yes, yes, since yesterday. Now listen good, sister. Meet me in front of the Ipanema Beach House.'

'Sure. Where is it?'

'Corner of Garcia d'Avila and Barao da Torre. It is not so far from your hotel.'

'Okay. When?'

'Soon as you can. And come alone. Alone! You understand?'

'Got it.'

'And remember, sister, trust no one.' The call ended.

I looked at the cell for a moment then tucked it away and turned to Juan-Carlos. 'Can you beat that?'

'What's she doing here, did she say?'

'Uh-uh. But whatever it is, she sounds scared out of her panties.'

'Where'd she want you to meet her?'

I hesitated.

'She told you not to tell anyone?'

I nodded. 'Not to trust anyone, either.'

'Protecting Danny.'

Silence. I knew he was waiting for me to reveal where I was going.

'I do trust you, you know,' I said lamely.

'But not enough to tell me where you're meeting her?'

I squirmed. 'Will you at least give me a few moments alone with her? You know. So I can tell who you are and why — ' I broke off, remembering that he was here to take my brother into custody and then deliver him to the D.A.'s office back home. 'I just thought of something — '

'Am I going to arrest Danny if he's with her?'

'Are you?'

'Of course.' When I didn't say anything, he said: 'You're thinking that if you tell

me, you're selling out your brother
again?'

'Bingo.'

'That's certainly one way of looking at
it.'

'You know another?'

'Well, you can always tell yourself that
if he's in protective custody with me —
Interpol — he's safe from Kazlov and his
thugs.'

'Until you turn him over to the D.A.'s
office. Then it's open season. He'd be a
target for every creep with a gun looking
to earn a fast buck.'

'The State Attorney promised me that
they'd keep him in a safe house till the
trial, and afterwards, bury him so deep in
the Witness Protection Program that no
one will find him.'

I turned the idea over in my mind.
How would Danny feel about such a
life-changing move? Starting life all over
again. New name. New city. New friends.
New everything. Basically, reinventing
himself. And maybe the hardest part of all
— never being able to tell anyone who
you really are or contacting anyone from

your past — including me, his sister and only living relative. The answer was simple.

'He'd hate it!'

'Who'd hate what?' Juan-Carlos said.

'Nothing,' I said. 'I was just thinking aloud.'

I turned my back to him and stared out the window, trying to give myself time to collect my thoughts.

'So, what's your decision?'

'I'm thinking, I'm thinking . . . '

I turned back to him. He had my watch in his hand. 'Here,' he said, offering it to me. 'Better put this on before you forget it. Leave it lying around and I'm afraid it'll have a new owner.'

'They're welcome to it,' I said. I took the cheap Rolex rip-off I'd bought especially to bring here, where kids on motor scooters are known to rip jewelry off a passing tourist's arm, and slid the band over my wrist. 'Ten minutes,' I said then. 'Ten minutes alone with Yolanda so she can tell me why she called and I can explain why I brought you along. Ten minutes. Then you're welcome to join the party. Deal?'

'Before I agree, I still have to take Danny into protective custody. You understand that?'

I nodded, thinking: Sure. I understand. I understand fine. The question is, will Danny understand?

And the answer to that was a big fat no!

7

Originally a private home, the Ipanema Beach House and its adjoining dorms was now basically a hostel for young tourists accustomed to back-packing their way across different countries. The corner it stood on was considered one of the hippest in town, the sun-splashed streets filled with nightclubs, shops, bars, cafés and trendy restaurants.

Juan-Carlos let me off one block before the corner then drove on to find a parking place. He'd promised to give me ten minutes to talk to Yolanda alone and hopefully learn where my brother was, but there was nothing I could say that would make him change his mind about taking Danny into protective custody.

Despite repeatedly telling myself that I was doing the right thing, for Danny and me, as I approached the corner I still felt guilty for agreeing to turn him in. But there really wasn't much else I could do at the moment — other than not show up. And I didn't want to let Yolanda down. For all I knew, her panic and wanting to see me might not be connected to my brother at all.

Sure, I thought sarcastically. And there really is a Santa Claus!

When I reached the old, two-story, gray-painted hostel, I paused on the tree-lined sidewalk and looked around for Yolanda. I couldn't see her anywhere. Student types, with sunburned faces and backpacks, hurried in and out of the front yard and entrance which was almost hidden by trees and tropical shrubs. I moved closer to make sure Yolanda wasn't standing on the steps. She wasn't. Nor was she among the young men and women gathered under the umbrella-shaded tables in the tiled courtyard. I watched them for a moment, their enthusiastic voices and laughter as they swapped adventures adding to the cacophony of honking cars, taxis, motor-scooters and trucks driving along the congested street behind me.

Five minutes passed and still no

Yolanda. I began to wonder if something had happened to her, or if at the last minute she had changed her mind about talking to me. I also wondered how much longer Juan-Carlos would wait before calling things off. I looked up and down the street but couldn't see him or his car.

Fifteen minutes passed. Still no Yolanda. I was getting ready to call it a day and start back to the hotel when a silver-blue Mercedes with dark tinted windows glided up. I turned toward it, wondering if it was delivering Yolanda.

It was — but not in the way I expected.

The curbside rear door swung open and her naked body was hurled out. It landed at my feet, limply, limbs flopping, head lolling from side-to-side like a broken doll. I screamed, the shrill sound mingling with the sweeping of tires as the driver gunned the engine and the car rocketed off, a man in the back seat desperately grabbing at the still-open rear door. He finally got it closed just as the car reached the intersection and, brakes screeching, skidded around the corner.

Almost immediately I heard rubber

burning as police cars came roaring up the street after them, sirens blaring as they weaved in and out of the traffic that had stopped or pulled over.

Other police cars raced past along the cross-street, Barao da Torre, after the now-disappeared Mercedes. Though I couldn't see what was going on, I heard gunfire beyond the buildings hiding the action. I heard more brakes screeching, then a loud crash, the grinding of metal against metal, more shots, some of them from automatic weapons — then silence.

The shootout seemed to last forever, but probably only took seconds. Before it ended I had already kneeled beside Yolanda, covered her naked, bruised and bleeding body with my jacket and now cradled her head in my arms.

Her huge dark eyes stared fixedly at me. They were filled with pain and possessed a vague questioning look, an emptiness that suggested neither they nor their owner had any idea what was going on. Her thick, bloodied lips cracked open as she fought to speak. I pressed my ear against them and heard her dying words:

'I . . . not tell . . . them anything . . . '

'Tell who?' I asked. Then when she didn't answer: 'Yolanda, talk to me . . . tell me who tortured you.'

'K-Kazlov's men . . . they want to know where D-Danny . . . is . . . but I not say . . . no matter w-what they do . . . to . . . m-me . . . '

I heard her last breath whisper out of her, a sound like the wind rustling through treetops, then she sagged and her head fell limply sideways. I didn't need to check her pulse to know she was dead. Inside, I wept for her.

As I stood up I saw Juan-Carlos appear around the corner and come running along the sidewalk toward me. He brushed aside the crowd of shocked onlookers that had gathered about me, waving his arms and ordering them in Portuguese to stand back!

'You all right?' he asked me.

I nodded numbly.

He knelt beside Yolanda. 'Did she say anything before she died?' he asked after he couldn't find her pulse.

'Something about not telling them

where Danny was even though they tortured her,' I said. The sight of all the cigarette burns, bruises and cuts on her body sickened me and I turned away, adding: 'Maybe my brother's got the right idea.'

'About what?'

'Running away from these people.'

Juan-Carlos straightened up and confronted me. His expression was a mixture of rage, concern and tenderness. 'That's exactly what they want. Their MO is — intimidation.'

'Well, they got my vote.' I squeezed my brows together. 'If it's all right with you, I'd like to go back to my hotel now. It's almost time for my pain meds and anyway, I need a drink — in fact a whole bunch of drinks.'

'I'll have one of the officers drive you. I insist,' he said as I started to protest. 'Just because these bastards are dead, doesn't mean their playmates aren't still around.'

That thought silenced all my protests. 'Will you be by later?' I asked.

'Try to stop me,' he said with a wry little smile.

It was the same smile I'd first fallen for and again the urge hit me.

'Think it'd be okay if I gave you a big wet kiss?'

He shrank back a little. 'Uh-hm, maybe not the best idea right now. But I'd love a rain check.'

I felt better then — safer. And though I'd lost a chance to perhaps find out where my brother was hiding, I had at least found a man whom I enjoyed being with; a man I felt I could trust with my life.

Juan spoke on his cell, ended the call and said: 'Car's on its way.'

I nodded. 'Did you get them all — the creeps in the Mercedes, I mean?'

'They're dead, if that's what you mean?'

'Good.'

'Would've been better if one had lived long enough to talk.'

I tried to think of a flip reply, but I was too bummed out about Yolanda.

Just then a police car ground to a halt beside us. A uniformed officer got out and opened the rear door for me. I nodded goodbye to Juan-Carlos and climbed in.

The officer got behind the wheel, fired the engine and pulled away from the curb. I was exhausted and mentally drained. It was only a few blocks to the hotel. But every time I leaned my head back and closed my eyes I visualized Yolanda's tortured naked body.

Emotionally it was the longest ride in my life.

8

Back in my hotel suite I stared at myself in the bathroom mirror. I looked like the beach at low tide. I was too tired to even bother to undress. I kicked off my shoes and flopped down on the bed, asleep almost before my head hit the pillow.

It was late-afternoon when I next awoke. I'd been dreaming about a giant gold fish that was eating the world and saving me for dessert while singing Christmas Carols and when I sat up I realized that despite the air-conditioning, I was soaked with sweat. I'm used to weird dreams now. And night sweats. My doctor warned me that my cancer medication had some side-effects, but that they often were different with each individual patient. Some patients had severe side-effects, while others only mild ones. None were beneficial, he'd admitted. But on the other hand, taking one pill a day was far easier on a patient than prolonged chemo-radiation treatments.

Having lost friends to cancers of various sorts, and seen how radically some of them changed after chemo-therapy — Dana's sister told me before she died that she often thought the 'cure was worse than the disease' — I considered myself damned lucky that the side-effects I was experiencing so far were the two I just mentioned along with bruising, feeling exhausted and weak at times and occasional bad stomach cramps. I mean how could I complain about that?

A knock on the door interrupted my thinking. Donning my robe, I went to the door and asked who it was.

'Hotel security wishes to speak to you, senhora.'

I recognized the gravelly voice of Sergeant Lucas Sousa, a policeman Juan-Carlos had assigned to guard me, and opened door. Sgt. Sousa nodded politely to me then moved aside, revealing the huge dark-skinned security guard who'd been with Juan-Carlos yesterday.

'I am sorry to disturb you, Senhora Hara — '

'That's okay,' I said, deciding to ignore his mispronouncing my name. 'What can I do for you?'

'I find this' — he held up a small diamond stud-earring — 'on the stairs by the rear exit of the hotel . . . same place I find your purse, senhora. I am wondering if it is yours.'

I was about to say no — that I didn't wear stud-earrings because my ears weren't pierced — when a thought hit me: 'May I see it, please?'

He gave me the earring. I studied it, turning it over between my fingers, wondering if fate had dealt me an ace. 'Hang on,' I told him. I got my purse from the counter, brought it to the door and tipped him eighteen Reais, which was about ten bucks. 'Here, that's for you. It's not mine,' I said as he started to thank me. 'But I'd like to show it to Senhor Albanez, if that's okay with you? It might have something to do with the man who attacked me.'

★　★　★

160

Juan-Carlos must have been close to the hotel because he arrived at my door within ten minutes. He looked rumpled and sexy in a white tropical suit and tan sport-shirt that set off his brown eyes, and seemed relieved to find me unharmed.

'What's wrong?' he demanded. 'Are you all right?'

'Sure. Why? Someone tell you I wasn't?'

'Sergeant Sousa said you had to see me right away. A matter of importance, he said.'

'What did you want me to call it — lust?'

'Jackie!'

'Oh, come on, Juan, lighten up, will you? It's bad enough that I got armed cops guarding me twenty-four seven without you treating me like the First Lady hitch-hiking in Afghanistan.'

He relaxed a little, rested his tanned hands on my shoulders and looked intently into my eyes.

'You saw Yolanda, what they did to her. Wouldn't you say that was cause for seriousness?'

161

That hit home. I nodded. 'Sorry.' I saw my reflection in his gorgeous dark eyes, felt jelly-kneed and gently pushed him away.

'Okay, here's why I wanted to talk to you.' I handed him the diamond earring and explained where it had been found.

'Go on,' he said.

'Well, it's a stretch, I admit, but what if the earring belongs to the guy who broke into my room? Security found it near where he ditched my purse. What if that's where he took off his ski-mask, figuring he didn't want anyone outside to think he was a robber, and at the same time somehow pulled off the earring? It's happened to girlfriends of mine, when they were at weddings and removed their veils, so . . . well, like I said, it's a long shot but — '

'I like it,' Juan said, cutting me off. 'Like it a lot. Good call, Ms. O'Hara. Talk about thinking on your feet.'

'Does that make me a candidate for Interpol?'

He chuckled, deep and throatily, then moved close, cupped his strong brown hands about my face and kissed me, hard on the lips.

'Hey, no fair,' I said as he stepped back. 'You're taking advantage of a sick woman.'

'Every chance I get,' he said. He looked at his watch. 'You're lucky that's all I have time for.'

'I don't call that lucky. You're really going?' I said as he went to the door.

'I must — unfortunately.'

'If you can leave me after a kiss like that, then you're a man with no heart.'

'Guilty as charged.' He took out a small plastic bag, dropped the earring inside and tucked the bag in his breast pocket. 'I'll let the manager know I've got this and that I need to run some tests on it.'

'Is that a good idea?'

'How else can I maybe get the wearer's DNA from it?'

'I meant, telling the manager. Like you once told me, security, the maids, the whole staff might be being bribed.'

He looked at me as if seeing me for the first time. 'What you said earlier — about being a candidate for Interpol — right now it's sounding like a really good idea.'

''Cept I may not be around for graduation.'

Sadness replaced his crinkly smile.

'I'll call you later,' he said. He pecked me on the cheek and was gone, the door closing quietly behind him.

'Atta girl,' I told myself. 'You really know how to kill a happy moment!'

9

At my request, room service delivered a pitcher of sangria and I spent the rest of the afternoon drinking it on the balcony and gazing out at the ocean. I'd asked them to make it potent, even if it meant doubling up on the red wine, and the bartender had responded with enthusiasm. Three glasses and I was feeling pretty good about life and halfway through my fourth glass, I swear some of the seagulls circling above the swimmers and body-surfers were performing loop-the-loops that would have made even Jonathan Livingston Seagull proud.

Gradually the sun went down. By now I was definitely not feeling any pain. I watched a bright-colored hang-glider drift lazily past and promised myself that I would try that and parasailing at least once before I flew home.

I didn't hear anyone enter my suite. I had my back to the door, my mind lost in the sound of the surf, and the first hint that I had company was when I felt hands grip my shoulders. Startled, I gave a tiny gasp and started to whirl around — only to have a black-gloved hand clamp a chloroformed cloth over my nose and mouth. My assailant's other hand locked around my chest, pinning me to the recliner.

I struggled frantically to break loose, at the same time trying to drag the hand away from my mouth. But it was hopeless. Whoever it was, they were twice my strength and I soon lost consciousness ... When I came around I was in semi-darkness and it took me a few moments to figure out my whereabouts. A sickly sweet smell in my nose reminded me that I'd been chloroformed. As my eyes grew accustomed to the dimness I saw I was sprawled on a bed in a small bedroom that was part of an RV or a camper. The vehicle was moving fairly fast. I listened and heard the sound of traffic outside. I guessed we were driving through a town or city, but not knowing how long I'd been unconscious I had no idea where we were. I sat up and realized there was duct tape covering my mouth and my hands were tied behind me. Obviously I'd been kidnapped. But why? And by whom?

I looked around for my purse, hoping I could use my cell to call Juan-Carlos. But my purse wasn't there. My feet weren't tied, so I swung them over the side of the bed and tried to stand up. I was weak-kneed from the after-effects of the chloroform, and lost my balance as the RV rounded a sharp corner. I tried to save myself but with my hands tied I couldn't grab anything and pitched forward, slamming against the wall then sliding to the floor. I sat there a few moments, waiting for the RV to straighten out and at the same time looking for something I could use to help pull myself up.

That's when the door opened. I looked up and saw a hulking figure silhouetted against the light in the adjoining living area of the RV. He wore a black woolen ski mask that hid everything except his eyes and lips, black gloves and sneakers and looked huge in dark, loose-fitting sweats. I was sure it was the same man who'd knocked me down and stolen my purse. I wondered who he was and why he'd kidnapped me, and if he'd had anything to do with torturing and killing Yolanda. I also wondered if he was connected to my brother — a drug dealer perhaps — or the Russian Mafia.

The latter seemed more likely. But if that was the case, why bring me here? Why risk being tailed by Interpol just to tell me something or punish me before killing me? Why not just kill me in my room? It wouldn't have been hard once my attacker got past my guard — which, by the way, was another equally puzzling question. How had my kidnapper gotten past Sergeant Sousa, who supposedly was standing watch outside my door?

A horrible thought hit me. Was Sousa dead? Had I indirectly caused the poor man to be murdered? I already felt vaguely guilty for Yolanda's death. Not that I'd asked her to come to Ipanema or contact me, but there was no denying that it was after she'd called me that someone

— Kazlov's men, presumably — killed her and dumped her naked body at my feet. And now maybe Sergeant Sousa was dead. Even as I thought that, I remembered what Juan-Carlos had told me about the Russian Mafia not considering me important enough to put out a contract on me; so why would they now have kidnapped me? It didn't make sense.

But if it wasn't the Russians, then who?

The big man moved from the doorway and stood over me. He eyes were almost as black as his mask. I could get no reading from them but his mere size alone was menacing.

'If you promise not to scream, senhora, I remove tape from your mouth.'

I nodded and tried to say 'I won't' behind the tape.

It sounded gurgled. But he must have understood because he pulled the tape off, and stood poised to gag me again if I tried to scream.

I didn't.

'Who are you?' I demanded. 'Why'd you kidnap me?'

He grinned, showing a gold front tooth

169

that looked familiar though I couldn't remember why, and scooped me up from the floor. For a moment I panicked. I like to consider myself a typically hard-nosed New Yorker, but facing rival advertising execs across a conference room table was a far cry from arguing with a masked kidnapper and the truth was I was really scared.

Then two things happened that helped calm my nerves: the man set me down on the bed and made no attempt to threaten or fondle me; and at the same time I suddenly remembered a magazine article I'd once read about kidnappers and kidnapping that said so long as the kidnapper kept their face covered, it indicated they didn't want to be recognized by their victim, which in turn suggested that for the time being at least the victim was safe. Since my kidnapper hadn't hurt me or removed his mask, I persuaded myself to believe that he didn't intend to kill me — for now.

'Where're you taking me?' I asked. Then, when he didn't reply: 'What do you want? If it's money, I'll gladly pay you whatever you ask. Just take me to an ATM — '

He cut me off, speaking rapidly in Portuguese.

'I can't understand you,' I said. 'I don't speak your language.'

'I say, senhora, it is not up to me what happens to you. I just do as I am paid to do and bring you here.'

'Then let me talk to whoever paid you, so I can tell them the same thing. Please,' I begged when he didn't answer. 'I'll pay you too if you want. Just get your boss. Tell him I want to talk to him.'

He studied me in grim silence and then he ran his tongue over his teeth — his gold tooth.

It suddenly hit me. 'You!' I blurted.

Instantly I regretted my blunder as first surprise, then anger narrowed his dark eyes. He then removed the ski-mask, revealing the face I'd already visualized: the dark-skinned security guard from my hotel.

At that moment I knew I was dead.

10

We drove through a labyrinth of narrow backstreets lined with impoverished buildings and shops. Poorly clad men and women crowded the sidewalks, while others talked and smoked in little sidewalk cafes, seemingly oblivious to the swarms of half-naked children playing in the dirt.

Now that I knew the identity of one of my captors, there was less need for secrecy. I was brought into the living-and-dining area and forced to sit on a bench seat, hands tied to the base of a fold-down table. The security guard, whose shirt nameplate read, N. Ruiz, sat opposite me, playing solitaire with a grimy deck of cards. I noticed his left ear was pierced, but had no earring in it. I couldn't remember if he'd been wearing an earring the first time I'd seen him, but I sensed the diamond stud-earring had been his and wondered why he'd brought it to me. Surely he knew that if his DNA was on it, it would eventually be traced back to him. It was all very puzzling.

The driver kept his back to us and from what little I could see of his face in the rear-view mirror showed wraparound sunglasses, a full auburn beard and tufts of reddish hair peeking out of his hooded sweatshirt. He never spoke so I could hear him. But occasionally he snapped his fingers, bringing Ruiz to his side. He then would whisper something, Ruiz would nod and return to his card game.

Two windows, one behind me, the other facing me revealed that we were driving through the heart of Rio, a sprawling city with an incongruous mixture of gleaming white skyscrapers and favelas — shantytowns made up of slum-shacks stacked one atop the other on the hillsides facing the dark, silvery-surfaced ocean.

I didn't know what time it was, but I guessed it was around ten or eleven o'clock at night. Neon lights lit up the darkness. We turned down Rua Cosme Velho, street signs directing us to Estacao de Ferro do Corcovado. As we slowed down on reaching the terminus of the Rack Railway to the top of the mountain, I glimpsed the moon beaming down on us. On any other night, it would have been romantic!

Presently we pulled into the parking area at the base of Corcovado Mountain, known throughout the world because of the giant statue of Christ the Redeemer at the summit. From all I'd read it was mobbed with tourists during the day and early evening; now, at this late hour, only a few vehicles were still parked there. Two-hundred-and-twenty-three steps led up to the summit. As we walked toward them, Ruiz with a gun jammed in my ribs, the driver limping ahead of us, I saw that the three view-elevators were closed for the night. But the escalator was still running and we headed for it.

I studied the driver as he stepped onto the shiny moving stairs, and saw that he was a little above medium height, wore a gray Nike tracksuit that had seen better days, scuffed sneakers and limped on his left foot. He looked bulky but I sensed he was wearing thick clothes under his sweatshirt to make himself appear heavier than he really was. He walked slightly stooped over, which made him seem shorter and older.

The last flight of escalators was not running. A printed sign read, FORADO DE SERVICO, which I presumed meant out of service. The three of us plodded upward. We were now over two thousand feet and were out of breath by the time we finally reached the café-level terrace. The yellow and green umbrellas that shaded the tables during the day were still up but the restaurant was closed. From here, wide stone steps led us up to the topmost viewing area that surrounded the gigantic black base of the statue. There were less than a dozen people standing by the parapet, gazing at the view. Mostly, they were young couples, lovers necking in the moonlight.

The three of us walked to the chapel in the base of the statue. It was locked but the driver used something to silently jimmy open the door and entered ahead of us. Ruiz prodded me inside and then closed the door.

The chapel was large enough to seat about one hundred-and-fifty people. It was dimly lit by rows of lighted candles behind the altar. I looked about me as we walked up one of the aisles, moved by the numerous scenes from the Bible and the paintings of Christ and Mother Mary.

But I didn't get to admire them for long: as soon as we reached the altar Ruiz forced me to my knees and took out a gun with a silencer.

'If you have any last prayers,' he growled, 'say them now.'

The driver moved off into the shadows before I could plead with him. I turned to Ruiz and implored him to tell me why he was going to kill me.

'To save the life of your brother, senhora.'

'I don't understand. How's killing me going to save Danny's life?'

'Because with you dead, he has one less enemy to worry about. You cannot betray him anymore.'

'I've never betrayed him,' I said desperately. 'What happened in Harlem wasn't my fault. I — '

'Mentirosa! You set a trap for him — so Dmitri Kazlov's men could kill him.'

'That's not true! I swear!' I included the driver, whose face was hidden by the shadows, adding: 'You've got to believe me.'

'Yolanda believed you,' Ruiz said bitterly, 'and she died at your feet.'

'What do you know about Yolanda?'

'Enough to know that she trusted you, called you to help her find your brother and you betrayed her — like you betrayed him.'

'No, no, I didn't. You've got it all wrong. I had nothing to do with her death. It was the Russian Mafia — Kazlov's men who killed her, not me. She told me so just before she died.'

'Enough! We're not interested in any more of your lies.' Ruiz pressed the silencer against the back of my head. 'Pray — ask God to forgive you your sins while you still have time.'

I was too scared to pray. But I sensed Ruiz would not pull the trigger as long as I was praying, so I pressed my untied hands together, closed my eyes and began murmuring under my breath.

It was strange. Though I did not want to die, there was a tiny part of me that was actually glad to get it over with. Once dead, there would be no more lingering, no more fear of the unknown, of wondering how ill I would get and how much I would suffer before the end finally came. Who knows, I thought. Perhaps this was Fate's kind way of sparing me all the potential pain.

I was wrong. Fate had other plans. Shortly, the driver left the shadows and walked past me, head lowered so I couldn't see his face, and headed up the aisle to the door. He muttered something over his shoulder to Ruiz, who promptly grasped my arm.

'Come. Get up,' he dragged me to my feet. 'Hurry!' He prodded me on along the aisle after the driver.

Though frightened, my Irish temper flared. I rebelled. Fear turned into rage. I'd be damned if I was going to hurry to my own grave. Whirling, I swung at Ruiz. He was too quick for me. He blocked my punch with his forearm, my watch taking the force of the blow, then pushed me away.

I glared at him. 'If you're going to shoot me, do it now.'

I was messing with the wrong man. Instantly, he pressed his silenced gun against my forehead and I knew by the cold flat look in his eyes that he fully intended to pull the trigger.

'No, not here!' the driver said behind me. He gripped me around the chest with one arm, and then reached around in front of my face and pressed duct tape over my mouth, silencing me.

At the same time Ruiz grasped my right wrist and twisted it roughly up behind my back, forcing me to submit or have my arm broken. He then herded me up the aisle after the driver.

Pain made my head swim. As I stumbled ahead of Ruiz I tried to recall the driver's voice. It was the first time he'd spoken loud enough for me to hear him and though I sensed he'd tried to disguise his voice, I knew it sounded vaguely familiar.

Outside, a cold wind had sprung up. It

came off the ocean, smelling of brine and seaweed, rustling the treetops on the mountain slopes below us. I looked around and realized everyone had left the viewing area. It was now up to me, and me alone to save myself. Optimistic as I usually am, I knew the chances of that were next to none.

11

The three of us walked to the parapet — a waist-high wall that ran around the entire viewing area, helping to prevent people from falling onto the steep, forested, rocky mountain slopes that disappeared into the darkness below.

The driver now turned to me. As he did the wind caught the hood of his sweatshirt, blowing it backward off his head. For the first time I saw his face — except it wasn't his face: on leaving the chapel he'd donned a thin rubber goblin mask that smiled grotesquely at me. Quickly pulling the hood back over his head, he nodded at Ruiz. 'Do it.'

Ruiz forced me up against the parapet so that I was facing the ocean and half-leaned over the wall. I realized then that he intended to push me over the parapet and watch as I plunged to my death. For an infinitesimal moment I stared down into the darkness, noticing as I did a large, bright yellow and red object resting on a narrow ledge just below the wall. Then the fear of death kicked in and I could think only of my survival —

'P-Please,' I begged. 'Don't do this. Please, I — ' As I spoke I kicked backward and upward with my right leg. It was a last-ditch effort to save my life and it worked. I felt the high heel of my shoe bury into Ruiz's groin. He grunted with pain, the grip on my wrist loosening as he stumbled back and doubled over, sucking wind.

I jerked free of him and spun around so that I was facing the driver. Momentarily he was caught off-guard and in that moment I grasped his mask and tore it off his face.

It's a moment I'll never forget.

The face staring at me in shock belonged to my brother, Danny!

I was equally stunned and speechless.

Before either of us could think of anything to say men came running up the steps — armed men, shadowy at first, then, as they got closer, clearly visible in their uniforms, until finally their faces became recognizable in the moonlight.

It was Juan-Carlos, Sergeant Sousa and several police officers.

I was so relieved I could have wept.

'Policia! Don't move!' Juan-Carlos shouted. 'Keep your hands where we can see them!'

For an instant neither Danny nor Ruiz moved.

Then my brother whirled and threw himself over the parapet —

At the same time Ruiz drew his gun and fired at the onrushing men.

I saw one of the officers stagger and fall.

'Get down! Get down!' Juan-Carlos screamed at me.

I obeyed.

As I dropped to the ground, Juan-Carlos and the police officers opened fire at Ruiz.

Hit, he staggered back, wobbled for a moment and then collapsed.

Juan-Carlos and the policemen came charging up.

'Get an ambulance,' Juan-Carlos told

Sergeant Sousa. 'Try to keep the sonofa-bitch alive!'

He then hunkered down beside me, slipped one arm under my back and helped me up. 'You all right, Jackie?'

I nodded. ''Yeah . . . I'm fine . . . '

'Sorry I didn't get here earlier. But for some reason the bug stopped signaling about five minutes ago, and we weren't sure exactly where you were.'

'Bug?' I said, surprised. 'What bug?'

He looked sheepish. 'In your watch,' he pointed. 'It's a tiny tracking device . . . kind of like a miniature GPS. I put it in there earlier today while you were — you know, 'cooling off' in the bedroom — '

'You bastard,' I exclaimed. 'Mean you knew where I was the whole time?'

'Up until a few minutes ago, yeah. Then, like I said, for some reason it stopped tracking.'

'Must've been when I tried to hit Ruiz,' I started to say — then I broke off, suddenly remembering my brother. 'Oh, my God — Danny!'

I ran to the parapet and looked over. I didn't know what to expect. But whatever it was, it wasn't what I saw:

Danny clinging to a bright red and yellow hang-glider, floating lazily out over the dark, forested mountainside below me. So that's what that object I'd glimpsed earlier was, I thought: a hang-glider!

'Yankee ingenuity,' Juan-Carlos said as he joined me at the wall. There was a tinge of admiration mixed in with his frustration of having lost a chance to arrest my brother, and despite everything I had to chuckle.

'That's Danny,' I said ruefully. 'If he'd put that kind of energy and brainwork into a profession, hell, there'd be no stopping him.'

'I need a chopper,' Juan-Carlos told one of the officers. 'Call your commander and tell him to try to pinpoint the suspect before he lands and disappears again.'

'Sim, senhor.' The officer quickly contacted his superior.

'Sir — ' Sergeant Sousa, who had been examining Ruiz, now joined us, looking grim. 'If you want to talk to him . . . better do it now. He hasn't got long.'

Juan-Carlos nodded. I went with him to Ruiz, who lay slumped against the wall, blood covering his chest. Juan-Carlos squatted down and put his ear to Ruiz' lips. Then he looked at up me. 'He wants to talk to you.'

'Me?' Puzzled, I knelt beside the dying man. 'What is it, Ruiz?'

His dark, blood-shot eyes stared fixedly at me. 'Y-Your brother . . . ' he said with great difficulty.

'Danny escaped,' I said. 'Had a hang-glider stashed over the wall. Got away clean.'

Ruiz went away for a moment, then returned and opened his eyes. I could see death in them and was surprised when he said: 'We — He only m-meant to . . . to frighten you . . . '

'Frighten me? What do you mean?'

'Weren't . . . we . . . were not g-gonna kill . . . you.'

'Really? Could've fooled me.'

'Would've sh-shot you . . . right 'way if . . . were, but . . . no . . . just tryin' to scare you . . . off.'

I frowned, not understanding. 'From

what — who — Kazlov's men?'

Ruiz's eyes closed. He didn't move. I couldn't see him breathing and thought he was dead. 'He's gone,' I said, turning to Juan-Carlos.

'So . . . you'd stop . . . ' Ruiz broke off again, and as I quickly turned back to him and saw he was still alive, he coughed up some blood before saying weakly, ' . . . following him,' and died.

Juan-Carlos felt his neck, could find no pulse and shook his head at me.

'Don't expect any sympathy from me,' I said. 'If you guys'd gotten here two seconds later, I'd be road kill somewhere down on the mountain.'

'I dunno,' Juan-Carlos said.

'Don't know what?'

'Ruiz might be right, you know.'

''Bout what? Quit talking in damn' riddles, will you?'

He ignored my vent. 'I find it hard to believe that a brother — even a brother like Danny — would actually kill his own sister. Someone who — from what the D.A.'s office assured me — loved you despite everything.'

I could see he was serious and that stopped me from snapping at him. But I had trouble getting my brain around it. All this time, kidnapping me, bringing me here, forcing me to pray under the threat of death, and then half-pushing me over the wall — all Danny was trying to do was scare me off?

'I know at first it doesn't make sense,' Juan-Carlos said, as if reading my mind, 'but you have to take into consideration that he actually believes you're out to kill him.'

'If the stupid jerk would only give me a few minutes to explain,' I began — then stopped as I realized Juan-Carlos had a point. 'You honestly think it's true?' I said. 'That all this was just a charade — scare tactics to make me stop looking for him?'

Juan-Carlos shrugged. 'I'm just saying it's possible — worth maybe considering. I mean he's the only brother you've got and though hopefully the doctors' prognosis is wrong . . . you might not . . . well, you know what I mean.'

Only too well, I thought.

'Look, I'll give it some thought,' I said grudgingly. 'Meanwhile, would you mind taking me back to the RV. My purse and everything in it are inside.'

12

After we'd collected my purse from the RV, which was impounded by the police, Juan-Carlos drove me back to my hotel.

As we were getting close to the ocean, my cell buzzed. I checked the caller ID, saw it was Kirk and answered.

'Hi, you.'

'Hi, Irish.'

'What's up?'

'Nothing. Just checking in. How about you?'

'Well,' I said, winking at Juan-Carlos, 'presently I'm being driven to my hotel by a hot looking 'gigolo' named Juan-Carlos Albenez.'

There was a long silence.

'Hello? . . . Kirk, you still there?'

''Course I'm still here.' He sighed wearily before adding: 'If you're trying to make me jealous — '

I laughed. 'I know you better than that.

Besides, Senhor Albenez is actually a very nice gentleman who is with — '

'Interpol, yeah, yeah, I know.'

'What you don't know, however,' I said tartly, 'is that I saw Danny tonight — just a little while ago in fact. Up on the top of Corcovado — you know, where that huge statue of Christ is?'

Kirk immediately became hyper — something he rarely does when he's talking to me. 'That's wonderful, Irish. Look, uhm, I'm sorry, but I gotta run. Something important just came up and . . . we'll talk later, okay?'

'But — ?'

'I'll call you, all right. Promise.' The line went dead in my ear.

I frowned and looked disbelievingly at my cell.

'What's wrong?' Juan-Carlos asked.

'Nothing.' I tucked the cell away.

'Then why the reaction?'

'Kirk . . . he just blew me off.'

'That's unusual?'

'More than unusual. I can't remember the last time it happened.'

'Maybe his girlfriend just walked in?'

I didn't answer. I was still trying to recover from Kirk's quick exit.

★ ★ ★

When we got off the hotel elevator and walked, hands clasped, along the hallway to my suite, there was a plainclothes police detective standing guard outside my door. His ID was displayed, the badge hanging from his breast pocket, and I noticed a distinctive bulge under his jacket.

'What's he doing here' I whispered to Juan-Carlos.

He shrugged. 'Must be your new watchdog.'

'Mean you didn't request him?'

'Uh-uh.' For an instant he frowned, as if troubled. Then he shrugged and smiled at the tall, stern-faced policeman. 'Officer, we won't be needing you any more tonight.'

'Sir?'

Juan-Carlos took out his Interpol ID and showed it to the detective. I saw respect cross the officer's face. He seemed to stand taller, straighter. 'Sim, senhor.' He nodded politely at me. 'Boa noite, Senhora O'Hara.'

'G'night,' I said. I watched him head for the elevator. 'Hmm. Nice ass.'

Juan-Carlos shook his head and sighed.

'Not as cute as yours, though,' I said. I swiped my card key in the lock, opened the door and waltzed happily into my suite.

It was filled with the fragrance of orchids. I turned the light on and saw the tropical blooms already in a vase on the counter, along with a bottle of Cristal champagne buried in an ice bucket.

'I see I have a rival,' Juan-Carlos said as I took the greeting card from among the orchids. 'Should I be worried?'

I chuckled and read the wording on the card aloud: 'Love ya. K.'

'For an ex-husband, he seems extremely devoted.'

'It's a two-way street,' I said, opening the slider to the balcony. 'We both care about each other.'

'Yet you're divorced?'

'Yep. And if truth be told, we wouldn't

have it any other way. Now,' I added, 'how about forgetting my ex- and opening that champagne? After all that's happened tonight, I could use about ten glasses.'

'Coming right up, senhora.' He bowed slightly and began untwisting the wire around the cork.

Out on the balcony I leaned against the railing and gazed at the midnight-blue ocean. The moon had whitened the rippling surface and each wave breaking on the sand resembled liquid silver.

I heard a cork pop and moments later Juan-Carlos joined me on the balcony carrying two glasses of bubbly. I turned to him, took the glass he offered me and clinked it gently against his.

'Cheers.'

'Saude.'

We both drank. The champagne went down cold and delicious, the bubbles faintly tickling in my nose.

'To the future,' he said, toasting me.

'The future,' I agreed, 'short as it is.'

We drank and then Juan-Carlos set his glass down and reached into his jacket.

'Unfortunately,' he said softly, 'it may

not be short enough.'

Puzzled, I looked at him. His expression had changed. His dark brown eyes had lost their warmth and his mouth had tightened into a thin, hard line.

I glanced down and saw the gun in his hand — a gun with a silencer attached to the barrel.

Stunned, I could only stare at him in disbelief.

'Why?' I asked when I could find my voice.

'Money,' he said. 'What else?'

'Kazlov?'

Juan-Carlos nodded. 'The Russians, they are low-class murdering pigs, but they pay well. Extremely well.'

For once I could not think of anything to say.

'I'm truly sorry,' he began.

A shot was fired. I jumped, startled.

Juan's eyes grew round with shock. He half-turned toward the living area. But he was dead before he could see who had shot him.

The gun slipped from his numb fingers. He crumpled, sideways, tried to grasp the railing, couldn't, and fell over it . . . disappearing from my sight.

I think I screamed.

'It's all right, Senhora O'Hara,' a voice said.

I turned as a man joined me on the balcony. It was my new watchdog, the plainclothes homicide detective with a gun in his hand. He brushed past me and looked over the balcony.

'I wouldn't,' he said as I also went to look. 'It is not pretty.'

I looked anyway. It wasn't. A small crowd was gathering around Juan-Carlos' corpse as it lay sprawled, face-down on the sidewalk. A dark stain that I knew was blood was spreading out from his head.

The detective tucked the gun into his shoulder holster and got out his cell. He speed-dialed a number. Returning to the living area, he turned his back to me and spoke quietly to someone.

On wobbly legs, I left the balcony and walked to the counter where I refilled my glass with champagne. As I sipped it I realized my hands were trembling. Up till then I had not heard what the detective had said. Now, he turned and looked at me, questioningly, and said:

'Sim, senhor, Senhora O'Hara is quite safe. Sim, senhor. Claro! Boa noite.' He ended the call and tucked the cell away.

'Who were you talking to?' I asked.

'Excuse me, senhora, but that is a police matter.'

'I see . . . ' I sipped my champagne, feeling calmer now — and a lot more curious. 'Humor me for a minute, will you, detective . . . but how did you know Juan-Carlos was going to shoot me? Or is that also a 'police matter'?'

The detective looked at me, long and hard. For a moment I thought he was going to tell me to mind my own business. Instead, he said: 'The Chief of Police received a call and notified Captain Branco — '

'Your boss?'

He nodded.

'Then he called you and you came galloping in to my rescue?'

The detective smiled. He had a nice, shy smile and I liked him a lot better when he was smiling.

'Please forgive me, senhora, but I must go downstairs now and make a positive identification of the corpse. Please, do not open your door to anyone while I am gone.'

'Scouts honor,' I said, adding: 'How will I know it's you unless I open the door?'

'I will announce myself.' He showed me his ID.

'Good enough.' I watched him hurry to the door. 'Oh, Detective Ribeiro — '

'Sim, senhora?'

'Thanks for saving my life.'

He smiled, shyly, and left. I locked the door behind him and stood there a moment, trying to make sense of all that had just happened.

Then it hit me. Going to my purse, I dug out my cell and called Kirk.

He answered immediately. 'Irish, I'm busy right now, so unless this is really important . . . '

'I'll only be a second.'

'Oh, all right. Go ahead. I'm listening.'

'Just wanted to thank you.'

'For what?'

'Always being there for me.'

'What?'

'See you soon, Mr. K. Love ya.' I ended the call. As I stood there sipping my champagne, hearing the surf pounding below on the beach, I realized that despite my medical situation I had so many blessings to count.

Part Three

1

The smell of fish entrails, on the docks in Shimoda, was making me queasy. I was jet lagged, sick from cancer meds and completely drained. I made my way to the marketplace trying to focus on one sound at a time. The voices, shouting a language I can't speak or comprehend, seemed to climb on top of one another, piling up inside my ears and making it difficult to focus.

My exhaustion began manifesting itself as paranoia and suspicion. I had been trailing Stephanie for two days and thought everyone she passed took an interest in her. I needed to make a move but knew if Stephanie was being followed then surely whoever was tracking her had discovered my arrival in Japan as well. Shimoda is a small town frequented by tourists, so a wandering American is not uncommon, but I wanted to get out of there as soon as possible and into Tokyo, where she and I could disappear more easily. Stephanie and my brother, Danny had been engaged before he disappeared but I'd never met her and wasn't sure whether she could be trusted.

I'm not a trained spy. Running a successful Manhattan ad agency does require a bit of undercover work, but mainly it consists of prying information from office assistants, CEOs and other industry execs, about my competition and what I might need to do in order to win a client. As for foreign travel, I'm accustomed to first class flights to luxury hotels or hitching a ride in my ex husband Kirk's private plane. I've eaten in the finest restaurants all around the world and now I'm slipping on fish guts and will be lucky to get some broth and a bowl of rice before the end of the day.

If Kirk Harmon could see me now he'd never believe it. Let's face it, if Kirk could see me now he'd scream multiple obscenities at my recklessness and probably find some way to have me kicked out of Japan, even if it meant trumping up fake charges to have me extradited, anything to have me back safely on U.S. soil.

I'd promised him if he would use his government contacts to track down Stephanie I'd leave it to the authorities to find her. Of course the minute he told me where she was, I was on a plane. It was my stubbornness that probably led to our divorce — that and the fact that I was never quite sure his business trips were strictly business and whether his business was strictly legal.

I'm not one to live suspiciously or ask too many questions, which makes my present situation that much more ironic. Sneaking around has never been my style; it reeks of desperation. However, things change and with life's clock counting down, all that matters is finding Danny, and if that means sneaking around and slipping on fish guts — bring it on.

From under my straw sun-hat I watched Stephanie Takeda, young, beautiful and graceful, make her way through the crowd. She seemed comfortable and relaxed. She was dressed in a floral silk wrap over a black, tight fitting t-shirt, loose black linen pants and traditional Japanese Geta sandals. I'd only seen her in photos and couldn't believe how gorgeous she was in person. It wasn't difficult to see what Danny had been drawn to. Being half Japanese and half Caucasian, she didn't blend in much better than me with my more than auburn, less than orange, Irish hair. She didn't have the same thick inky-black hair as the Japanese. Hers was waist-length, the shade of cocoa powder and was streaked with golden highlights. Her almond shaped, light brown eyes were streaked with ribbons of green. She'd be considered exotic in any nation.

As I got closer I realized she was speaking fluent Japanese, which pleased the merchants. My fears lessened as I began to understand it was her uniqueness that was drawing attention, not her connection to Danny, Kazlov or Interpol. As the thought left my mind I couldn't help but marvel at the state of my life. How did all this get so out of control? The Russian mob? Interpol? These were organizations featured on the History

Channel or movies-of-the-week, not from in my life.

Stephanie stopped at a vendor and I decided I needed to make her aware of my presence. I casually stopped at the same vendor and perused the stacks of textiles. She looked up and smiled and startled me as she spoke.

'Two days is quite an investment of time. I assume you didn't get all the info you needed if you're making yourself known.'

'I'm sorry?' I asked, startled by her abruptness.

'I'm not new to this you know. I've gotten used to being followed. I will tell you the same thing I tell all the rest. I don't know where he is, I don't care and I have nothing to offer.'

I am not prone to speechlessness and I'm really not used to being taken off guard. I'm usually very much in control. So far, this encounter was not starting out as I'd planned and I didn't like it. I scrambled mentally to regain the edge I'd come to rely on. 'Hey stand down. Just who do you think I am?'

She looked up at me with a bored expression. 'I really don't care who you are, or who you work for. It's of no concern to me.'

With that she turned and walked away. A bit dumbfounded I chased after her.

'Stephanie! Wait!'

She stopped, looked around then turned to face me. 'Please don't make a scene. I'm trying to build a life here and I don't need people gossiping. The town is small and you are not as subtle as you think. You might as well carry a sign that says 'stupid American.''

I gave her credit for blowing my cover and calling me out so easily, but her flat-out disrespect was irritating me and I was quickly losing my patience. I was used to tough women. Being a female CEO, you often rub elbows with other highly successful, high-profile women and we all seem to have a little bit in common. We've all learned to paint a veneer on ourselves, polished and hard, and if you want to know what's underneath you need to come at us with a chisel. From the onset, Stephanie very much reminded me of one of my professional counterparts, but just before I could respond I noticed something. She'd reached up to grasp the knot of her scarf and her hand was trembling, not much, but enough to betray her. She was bluffing.

I softened. 'Look, Stephanie, I don't know who you think I am, or what it is you think I'm after, but you're making a big mistake. I'm here to help you. You're in danger.'

'Ha! That's funny. Did you come all the way from the States to tell me this? Listen, love, you're wasting your time. I knew my days were numbered the minute I woke up and saw that Danny had bolted. So unless you're here to kill me, you'd better just get yourself back home.'

2

I should know by now to stop ordering my steps. My plan for confronting Stephanie hadn't gone according to my design, which shouldn't be so surprising. Lately, nothing in my life had been going according to my plans. Control freaks everywhere should get a taste of the uncertainty I've experienced over the last several months of my life. Being shot at by Russian mobsters, and being told you have cancer, tends to peel, finger by finger, the firm, white-knuckle grasp we think we have on life.

I was able to convince Stephanie to get a cup of tea with me. Given the way our encounter had begun I was surprised she conceded without much resistance. She simply agreed, saying she was about to get some tea anyway, so she'd give me a few minutes of her time. As if I'd come all this way to sell her life insurance.

I started with a brief explanation of my

motives intending to soothe her nerves and convince her I wasn't there to kill her. To my monologue she replied, 'No offense love . . . ' The way she called me 'love' reminded me of the wealthy, middle-aged women from Park Avenue. I assume people who say it think it sounds refined. It was annoying and I'd already planned on letting her know once we got to know each other better. She continued: ' . . . but I never really thought you were here to kill me.'

I knew I shouldn't be bothered that she didn't take me for a coldblooded killer, but I didn't like the fact that she didn't think I'd have the nerve. There are certain qualities people typically hope to own — characteristics people often ascribe to themselves with pride. For instance: good driver, cool under pressure, high pain threshold, able to pull the trigger if cause should arise; you know, your typical unflappable, no nonsense, take-charge-kind-of-person, attributes. The fact that she didn't think I was made of tough stock got on my nerves.

'Glad to hear it,' I said exasperated.

'But there's something you have to know. Look Stephanie, I'm Danny's sister.'

Shock immediately spread across her face. 'Jackie? But how ... I mean ... what ... ?'

'Yep, Jackie O' in the flesh, and if you're finished with your claws, do you mind putting them away for a bit so we can talk?'

'But what ... ? How did you ... ?' She was struggling to put the pieces together.

This is more like it, I thought. For the first time since coming into contact with her I'd found my footing. I was back in control.

'It would appear you're not much better at this cat and mouse game than I am. It wasn't that hard to find you if that's what you're trying to figure out.'

She raised an eyebrow and waved off my jab. I don't know what she intended, but I took the gesture as a surrender of sorts. She elegantly sipped her green tea from the small heavily glazed, baked clay teacup. Her long fingers cupped it gently and the off white color made it look like she was cradling a pearl. I sipped my tea and felt my shoulders relax. The sound from a bamboo flute sauntered through the teahouse, and I took a moment to size-up Stephanie.

She seemed way out of Danny's league. I wasn't sure I understood what she'd seen in him. I love my brother and all, and I'm fully aware that, since the instant he crossed the line into puberty, he's never had to look for attention from the opposite sex; but this pairing seemed unlikely. He has a swagger girls can't seem to resist. And though it's been awhile since I've had the pleasure of meeting any of the women from the undoubtedly long list of companions he's kept warm at night, I remember his type: big hair, bigger boobs, tight low-cut shirts, tight pants and bright lipstick, the complete opposite of the woman sitting across from me.

Stephanie seemed to be a woman of class. Refined. She didn't seem to be the type to fall for his mischievous grin, carefree demeanor and partying ways. I was dying to find out just what on earth she had seen in my brother.

'I can't believe you're here,' she said, breaking the silence. 'Danny's beloved sister.' She spoke with a slight bitterness but it wasn't directed at me; rather it seemed to be directed at her memories of her time spent with Danny.

'Beloved? That's cute. I don't feel very beloved.'

'He's not very good at expressing his true feelings I suppose. But honestly, the way he spoke of you . . . ' she paused and a very small smile spread across her face, 'the way he spoke of you was one of the reasons I fell in love with him. It was part of why I trusted him.'

'I'm sorry to say this, but I think he was probably manipulating you. I'm not sure I've ever been that high on his list.' I debated whether or not to tell her he'd stolen $100,000 from me. I wasn't sure how chummy I should get with her. I've seen enough chase movies to know the number one rule — Trust No One. 'We were really tight as kids and even closer after our mom died, but things went sour after our lives, how should I say it — took different paths I guess.'

'I'm sure his . . . ' she paused and I realized we were both choosing our words very carefully, neither of us wanting to say the wrong thing or admit to too much. Our encounter was as delicate as the tea set. She smiled sweetly: 'I'm sure his habits were of some detriment to your relationship.'

I decided to just put it out there: 'You mean the drugs.'

'Yes, I didn't want to just come out and say it in case you didn't know. But his drug use was severe. Drugs convince you your horrible choices are some of the best choices you've ever made.'

'Stephanie, you don't have to answer this, we've just met and I know we're both trying to be careful, so careful in fact that it's exhausting me, but were you two using together? I'm just trying to figure out how the two of you worked.'

She put her cup down and hung her head like the memory she was about to reveal was a mixture of embarrassment and possible shame.

'Not in the beginning. Actually, I was working as a model when I met Danny. I was quite busy, getting work all over the world. I'd gotten my life together and was reaping the benefits. My career was really taking off.'

'Let me guess, then you met Danny?'

'Well, to be honest it wasn't all his fault. When I first arrived on the scene I'd gotten really caught up in the thrill of it all. I was living in New York, and it was the first time I'd ever lived away from my parents. It was all so new and so exciting. I noticed a lot of the other girls were able to keep up with the pace better than I could, or so it seemed, anyway. They appeared to have energy to spare and never seemed to give food a second thought. One of the girls turned me on to their secret for success — lots and lots of drugs, speed, cocaine, some of them were even smoking crack. I was scared to death at first but wanted so much to be a part of that life . . . '

She began to tear up.

'Stephanie, you don't need to divulge all of this. I'm just searching for answers so I can understand who my brother has become and figure out how to reach him.

I'm not looking to dig up your demons.'

'No, it's okay. It feels good to get it out in the open.'

I decided to take advantage of her need for a good cathartic spilling of the guts, hoping she might slip up and give some information I could use to find Danny.

'I lived the life for quite a while,' she said, 'but gradually I realized that the girls who were the most successful were not engaging in the same lifestyle as me. They seemed fresh when they arrived at a shoot or show. They had more going for them than partying and praying for the next job. They were professionals. I started taking notes on some of their choices and decided I needed to make some changes. I started with the drugs. I immediately cut myself off — cold turkey. Fortunately I wasn't using anything too regularly. I was still just a weekend party girl so it wasn't a situation of withdrawal and the illness that can come with that. I still went out with the girls, clubbing on the weekends, hitting the newest bars and restaurants. Some of us even got paid to make appearances. I learned to cut myself off after one drink and switch to club soda and cranberry juice for the rest of the night. The change was incredible. I felt amazing.'

'So then why on earth would you ever have hooked up with my brother?'

'Believe me, I ask myself everyday why I didn't run when I had the chance.'

'Did you know he was using when you started dating?'

'No, but I don't know if it would have mattered. He was everything I was looking for and didn't even know I needed. He was generous and joyful. He brightened every room he entered and the way he spoke of the life we were going to build — were building — together was enough to sell me on him for good.'

'Where did you meet?'

'In the bar of Tormentare, downtown, Manhattan.'

I knew the restaurant. They approached me to do work for them before they opened, or at least their lawyers did. The whole thing was shady and I eventually cut ties with them. I couldn't get them to ever acknowledge who the real owners were. I was told, 'You're on a need-to-know basis Ms. O'Hara,' one too many times. I heard the finished project was beyond spectacular, and the list of wealthy, famous and beautiful that crossed its luxurious doorstep was immense.

She went on: 'I saw him watching me from across the room. He wasn't intimidated when our eyes would catch; he just kept his gaze fixed on me. Finally he walked over, put a hand on my waist and whispered in my ear, 'I would take care of you, keep you safe, protect your heart and serve you all the days of my life.' Then he kissed my cheek and walked away. I think I resolved to marry him right then and there.'

She enjoyed the memory for a short time before she continued. 'I knew it was a line, of course. I've heard thousands, but never like that. Such confidence that man has. I didn't care if it was true. I wanted the chance to make it true. I left with him that night and never looked back.'

Amazing, utterly amazing, I thought. Of course being his sister, and having known him longer than anyone, I assumed immediately that he'd ripped that touching sentiment from a Hallmark card or maybe he'd heard it in the vows at a wedding and tucked it away for future use. But I have to admit; I was touched at how deeply she'd been moved by him. It was clear she had some serious daddy issues and needed some good ol' fashioned caretaking. Unlucky for her, my brother's greatest gift has always been finding out a weakness and pressing his thumb on it until you cry uncle. How on earth he knew Stephanie's weakness before they'd ever met was beyond me. I suppose he's just gifted that way.

'That first night we played a flirty game of twenty questions.' She laughed at the memory and I cocked my head in curiosity hoping she'd divulge more. 'You know,' she said, answering the quizzical look on my face, 'questions like: Do you sleep naked or in pajamas, breakfast or just juice, modesty or exhibitionism — just playful, get to know you better, dating inquisition. However, about half-way through I asked him, 'drugs, alcohol, or cigarettes?' to which he replied 'no thanks, I'm good.' When I told him I was serious he said: 'I drink like a fish, but I stay clear of drugs. I've been there, done that and it wasn't good.' That was all I needed to hear. We were together everyday after that.'

'Do you think he was really off drugs back then?' I asked, because I knew Danny had experienced moments of sobriety.

'I don't really know. It seemed like he was being honest. He truly was a completely different person from the man he became. Back then I couldn't imagine him abandoning me and leaving me to fight for myself against Kaslov. Protect me? Hah, that's a laugh. He'd slowly started using again and I'd occasionally join him. I hate that I was so willing to follow him down the rabbit hole, but I was in love.'

'Like you said, drugs make dumb decisions seem really, really smart. But I'd have to agree with you. I remember that guy, the guy he was before he was strung out. He was an unstoppable force.

It's such a waste. You know, you're not the only one he's let down and abandoned. I'm right there with you and I think we need to get out of here if we want to keep ourselves safe and find Danny. He needs help, and we need to get to Tokyo, where we can disappear.'

'I'll go with you to Tokyo to keep myself safe, but don't think for a second I'll do anything to help that snake. I'll never forgive him.' In her pause I could see she didn't even believe herself. 'What makes you think he's here anyway?'

'You're here, so if what you said about how he had felt about you is true, I'm hoping he's here somewhere.'

She looked at me with an earnest expression, an almost sympathetic down-turned smile. 'I'm sorry to say this Jackie, but it sounds like wishful thinking.'

'Right now, wishes are about the only hope I have.'

3

We got off the train in Tokyo. I immediately felt safer amidst the buzz of metropolitan life. Tokyo is bright and loud like New York, but tamer. There was traffic and crowds but an overriding sense of calm and serenity that just isn't found on the streets of Manhattan. Unlike the hyped up citizens of New York, the people weren't pushing and bumping on the sidewalks. No one was hanging off the curb waiting for the light to turn; as though standing five feet from the curb will force the hand of the oncoming cars or traffic signals. We're all in such a hurry.

I was grateful for my small victories. Finding Stephanie proved to be a two-fold win. I now had a translator and a partner. I'm a seasoned international traveler, but regardless, having someone to read street signs and talk to the natives is never unwanted. After all, I wasn't there for a vacation.

Before coming over I knew I needed to make some arrangements. I created a fake email address and used it to open an anonymous online payment service linked to off-shore monies Kirk had provided for me years ago. As far as I knew he's the only one who ever knew it existed and since it didn't come up in the divorce I assumed he forgot about it. I rented an apartment anonymously through a vacation rental site and paid from the online account. I'd done my due diligence; I just prayed it was enough.

We made our way through the busy streets and found a bus depot. Neither of us was thrilled with the style of travel we'd succumb to but were fearful of leaving tracks. Taxi drivers would remember two Americans, especially one that was as beautiful as Stephanie who spoke Japanese perfectly and another with red hair and fair Irish skin. If the driver were questioned he'd have no reason not to deliver someone right to our doorstep, especially if pressured.

We traveled lightly, bringing one carry-on sized travel bag each, and a good map. We got to the apartment late in the evening. It was a quiet neighborhood with small two- and three-story apartment buildings. It was dark on the street and very few lights were on in neighboring houses. I was grateful for the cover of darkness and was eagerly anticipating the warmth of a soft bed. In Shimoda I'd paid a fisherman to let me sleep on his boat. The negotiations bordered on comical, think charades without the bowls of popcorn and family members shouting guesses.

We dropped our bags on the floor and Stephanie immediately headed for the kitchen. The whole apartment was white. White furniture, walls, kitchen cabinets and countertops — it was the epitome of sterile. The flooring was hard wood the color of bamboo. I felt fresher just walking in the door.

'Tea,' Stephanie said. 'I'm in desperate need of tea.'

I smiled weakly. The stress and travel had taken its toll. I rifled through my bag and grabbed my pill bottle.

'Are you ill or something?'

'Something like that.'

'Why on earth are you risking your health, your life, traipsing all over Japan, quite possibly, while people chase you?'

'My health is shot anyway, what do I have to lose?'

'Well, you're certainly not going to recover utilizing this method.'

'I'm not going to recover racing all over Manhattan either, or Africa, or Europe or Wyoming for that matter.'

'You mean you're really sick, dying?'

'Take it easy with the d-word,' I said, swallowing my pills and sinking into the couch. 'I don't like to say it out loud. And anyway, who knows, I may just beat this.'

I felt bad just dumping the news on her like that. I can be insensitive at times with the information. I enjoy the look on people's faces when they realize they're speaking to a potentially dead woman. I like their speechlessness. Stephanie paused to take in the situation and continued with her tea.

'I'm truly sorry.'

'Don't sweat it — it's not your fault.'

'Is that why you're so eager to find Danny?'

'Among other things.' I picked up a cushion from the couch and hugged it to my body. 'I actually told him. It was horrible. I caught up with him back home and explained my situation but before he even had time to process it we were being shot at. He started screaming at me. He thought I'd set him up for stealing money from me.'

'That's awful. That's awful for both of you.'

'Stephanie, it's very important that you not contact anyone while we're here. No one can know. If someone is tracking you via your cell phone, we're all in trouble — you, me, and I know this probably doesn't matter to you, but Danny too.'

'Of course. I know I talk as though I hate Danny, but I still care about him. I hate him for what he did to me, but I would never want to see him hurt. Do you have a plan? We can't just sit here hoping not to get killed.'

'Right now my plan is to shower and get myself to bed. The rest we can work out tomorrow.'

'Sounds good.'

I got up and headed to the bedroom I'd be staying in.

'Jackie?'

'Yeah?'

'I really am sorry about . . . well about everything.' I knew by everything she meant all of it, the cancer, Danny, the way she'd treated me earlier, every crappy thing I'd experienced up to that point. And even though we barely knew each other, her sympathy felt good. I knew I needed to be careful — needing sympathy was not a good thing.

'Thanks.' I said.

I was grateful that Stephanie seemed to understand the importance of my journey. I was beginning to really like her and found myself wishing she and Danny had begun their life together under different circumstances. She loved him. Or at least she was trying to convince me she did. And though with Danny it's hard to sort fact from fiction, it sounded as if he loved her too. I hoped that love was enough for him to follow her to Japan.

I got in bed, preparing myself for another night of nightmares. Being chased in your dreams night after night, just to awake and face the chase during the day is exhausting. As I lay there I thought about Stephanie's story and realized I was hungry for a connection to my brother. At first, I convinced myself that I was drawn to her story because there was the possibility I might discover useful information. However, the more she spoke, the closer I felt to Danny. I began to reminisce about our childhood. I remember cuddling up next to him at our mother's funeral and holding his hand at our father's just two years later. As much as I hated to admit it, I was looking for him for my benefit just as much as his.

I looked around the room, more white — white sheets, white bedspread, white dresser, white walls. It was cleansing. I fell asleep and rested peacefully for the first time in two days.

4

I awoke to Stephanie's alarmed shout coming from the living room. 'Jackie!'

I jumped out of bed and bashed my shin into the dresser. I knew immediately there'd be a nasty bruise, just another lovely side effect of the treatment. I raced into the living room. 'What is it?'

She was holding a slip of paper and was visibly shaken.

'What is that? What does it say?'

'Here, I think I'm going to be sick.'

She stuffed the paper into my hand and threw up into the toilet. My practical side is hard to quell and I immediately thought, 'There goes our sterile living environment.' I looked at the slip. It was a small piece of paper with a torn edge. All it said was, Get out of Tokyo.

'Where could this have come from Stephanie?'

'I haven't a clue,' she said, wiping her mouth on a cloth. 'I just came into the living room and saw it on the floor. Someone stuck it under the door.'

'If you don't know who it's from, why are you freaking out like this? You weren't this scared when you thought I was following you to kill you?'

'I already told you, I knew you weren't going to kill me. I assumed you were Interpol — they're the ones who've been harassing me. So far those gangsters Danny is running from haven't bothered me. That's why I came to Japan. I figured they wouldn't come this far just for me.'

'Somehow, someone knows we're here.' As I spoke I noticed Stephanie's phone on the counter. 'Did you make a call?' She looked back at her phone and back at me.

'No! I swear!'

'Stephanie, I'm serious, did you call someone?'

'No! I had it out to use as a flashlight in the middle of the night for water and to check the time. I swear I didn't call anyone.' I didn't know her well enough to know if she was lying or not. I wanted to trust her but still didn't know if I could.

I'm always a bit leery of anyone associated with my brother.

'OK, let's not panic. Let's figure out who could have done this and who would have motive.'

'I don't think it's Interpol,' she said. 'I've unfortunately had to deal with them quite extensively and this isn't their style.'

'Maybe they're changing things a bit,' I said with a hint of sarcasm.

'When I told you in Shimoda that I wasn't new to this, I was referring to Interpol. I've answered so many questions that I can't keep anything straight anymore. Even information I was sure of is now clouded. They would ask me a question and then ten minutes later ask the same question again, and then ask it again ten minutes after that, perhaps phrased in a slightly different way. It's terribly confusing and exhausting. I just don't see them slipping notes under doors.'

'No, I suppose you're right. My experience with them has been similar to yours; it's as though they're trying to cause me to trip on my own words hoping to somehow prove I know where Danny is. It's ridiculous. If they followed me for any length of time it would be clear that I'm as much in the dark about his whereabouts as they are.'

'Well,' Stephanie said plainly as though her forthcoming response was the most obvious and natural conclusion, 'I think we should do what the note says and leave Tokyo.'

I thought this was an odd response from a girl who seemed to be so in control only a day earlier in Shimoda. Allowing an anonymous threat to force her hand didn't seem to fit her personality.

'Look, I know I have less to lose than you. I'm living on borrowed time here, but I'm not going to be chased away until I'm good and ready to go.'

'Jackie, I'm not worried worry about being chased, I've been chased for quite some time. At this point, I'm concerned by the chasing — my chasing Danny. Actually, I'm worn down by it. I've chased your dear brother into more trouble than I care to admit. At this point

I see my leaving as heeding what sounds like wise counsel.'

I couldn't argue with her on that point, but I wasn't buying it either. If she really felt that way it wouldn't have been so easy to convince her to leave Shimoda. I wasn't sure just what her motives were but I was determined to find out.

Banking on the fact that her next move wasn't completely decided, I chose to work on her sympathies. I knew there had to be some reason for her coming with me to Tokyo and maybe her softer side would be my ticket in. Danny wasn't the only manipulator in the O'Hara family.

'Stephanie, I need your help. I know I have no right to ask but I'm sick and I can't do this alone. Danny has no one on his side, we have to help him.' I didn't want to admit it, but everything I was saying was true. I needed all the help I could get. I just hoped she was sensitive enough to cave in to my plea.

Exasperated, she finally spoke. 'What is it with you O'Haras? I can't seem to keep myself out of harm's way whenever anyone from your family is present.'

Relieved at her concession, I laughed. 'Yep, finding trouble is what we O'Hara's do best.'

'You guys should find another way to get your thrills.'

5

The mood in the apartment lightened,
but something about Stephanie wasn't
settling with me. She was calm and
composed but it seemed to be a forced
effort. Just like convincing her to leave
Shimoda for Tokyo, convincing her to go
forward with our search was easier than it
should've been. I know when someone's
putting on a show.

I decided it was imperative that I keep
her close. It was clear to me that she had
as much a reason for being here as I had
for wanting her here. Evidently we were
using one another and neither of us was
being completely honest about why. I
needed her for information and she
needed me for . . . well, that was the
$10,000 question. But you know what
they say about keeping your friends close
and your enemies closer. And since I
couldn't tell which camp she resided in, I
planned on doing everything I could to

keep her right by my side.

I enlisted her help in creating our game plan. I was hoping some of her insight might produce clues about what she knew, but I was also unsure about where to start and needed her knowledge of Japan and of Danny's last several months.

'Perhaps,' she interjected, 'we should wait until this evening before we get started. Knowing Danny he'll probably sleep until noon anyway and won't be getting out until after sun-down.'

'Any suggestions on where he may go? Does he have any contacts here? Who does he know in Japan?'

'Hmm, I'm not really sure. I have family all over Japan but as far as I know Danny didn't know anyone here.' She took a minute as a thought began to materialize. 'Wait, my cousin Toshi had business that brought him to New York frequently. He recently purchased an apartment in Chelsea and was only coming home to Japan once a quarter.'

'Did Danny know this?'

'Yes, he and Toshi were becoming quite close. Toshi appreciated the — how shall I put it — party favors perhaps, that Danny could provide. Danny could accommodate Toshi's needs when entertaining visiting business associates.'

'Ahh, I see. How professional.'

'Yes, well it would appear that some frat boys become frat men, always looking for the next party.'

'A little business mixed in with a lot of pleasure I assume.' I immediately thought of Kirk and all the 'out of town associates' he entertained. 'How nice of Danny to help your cousin out.'

'Yes, wasn't it.'

'Do you think Danny could be hiding out at Toshi's?

'Yes, I suppose it's possible.' She seemed reluctant to acknowledge the fact. 'But if we have figured this out don't you think everyone else has too?'

She was beginning to backtrack but it was too late. Mentally I was already at Toshi's place. 'Sure,' I said, 'I guess it's possible that everyone knows about Toshi, but didn't you say you had family all over Japan. Why would anyone pick Toshi out specifically?'

'Because, as I told you, we frequently spent time together.'

'But that was before anyone cared. There's no way anyone could know every single person he ever associated with. No one was following him then.'

She didn't fight me. 'Good,' I said, 'we'll head to Toshi's tonight. Where does he live?'

She took a deep breath that sounded like resignation. 'Tokyo.'

'Perfect!'

'Yes,' she said, sounding unconvinced, 'perfect.'

We decided to stay put until dark. We ordered food from a local grocer who delivered and tried to relax.

I was feeling enthusiastic and hopeful about finding Danny at Toshi's, but my concern about Stephanie's loyalty was growing. She was doing her best to appear as a woman self-possessed. But like a novice poker player, her tells were glaring. She was not the steel framed woman I'd met earlier. She made at least four pots of tea, twisted and untwisted her hair into a knot a half dozen times, and gently rubbed her fingertips over her cuticles mindlessly and incessantly.

'I'm not so sure this is such a good idea,' she finally ventured.

'Yeah, I picked up on that. You're not exactly buzzing with confidence.'

She was not amused by my observation. 'Discovering mysterious notes under my door — a door, may I remind you, that no one is supposed to know is mine — has the ability to rattle my composure. I'm just afraid the minute we walk out that door someone will be waiting to shoot at us.'

I decided as difficult as she was I liked her better on the docks in Shimoda. I wasn't fond of this current display of weakness. I wondered if it was genuine. Was she really frightened, or was this a ploy to steer us in a different direction? She was clearly worried but I wasn't exactly sure as to why.

'I think if I wanted to kill two women, I wouldn't warn them to get away. I don't know who left that note, but I don't think it was left by someone who wants to kill us.'

'Well, it was left by someone who is angry about us being in Tokyo and I don't want to upset the wrong people.'

'What are we going to find at Toshi's, Stephanie?'

'What? What on earth is that supposed to mean?'

'I'm getting the feeling that you might know what's waiting for us over there.'

'Nonsense. Of course I don't know what we'll find there. And don't forget I'm the one who suggested we go there. Why would I suggest it if I wasn't willing to go?'

'I don't know. Why don't you tell me?'

She stood up and put her hands on her hips. She immediately shed the anxiety and appeared to be in control once again.

'This is childish. We're exhausted and have a potentially trying evening ahead. Let's just get some rest.' With that she headed to her room and shut the door.

I couldn't help but smirk. I wasn't sure what was going on, but I was confident the night wouldn't end without finding some answers.

I walked over to her room and yelled through the door, 'Oh and, Stephanie, remember, stay off the phone.'

'Back off, Jackie.'

I knew the comment was unnecessary. But I wanted her to know I sensed a breach in our understanding. I may be new to this, but I'm no idiot.

6

Stephanie and I pored over maps and train schedules. We decided that instead of using the cover of night to make our move we'd use rush hour traffic. I wanted to be lost in a crowd.

If the train arrived on time, the trip would take less than 45 minutes. We decided that once we got to Toshi's we'd wait for dark. We'd hide out in a nearby shop, or even in the bushes if we had to.

As we headed out the door my heart was pounding, adrenalin can be powerful. I was hopeful. I even allowed myself a bit of a naïve excitement about reuniting with Danny, envisioning the three of us sipping tea and catching up. I longed for a normal relationship with my brother. I had faith this illness wouldn't take me anytime soon, but I didn't want to risk it either. I wanted to see him happy and healthy before I died.

Stephanie looked over her shoulder as

we headed down the hallway. She fidgeted anxiously as we made our way into the crowded Tokyo streets. She was looking for someone.

'You're drawing attention to yourself, just relax.' I needed her to get a hold of herself.

'I feel like we're being followed,' she said.

'We're just two girls out for a nice dinner. We're not on the run. We're not in any trouble.' I'm not great at soothing people's nerves. I knew I'd wasted my words. She didn't believe me. I didn't believe me.

The streets were filling with pedestrians. Restaurants and cafés were busy with men and women making their way home from their long workdays. Life was taking place all around us. It felt normal. But normality was no longer an option for me. Normalcy would forever be a foreign country — a country I was no longer a citizen of. Normal was people rushing around busy streets, picking up dinner on the way home from work. I'd taken a left at normal when I exited the hospital with a cancer diagnosis and committed myself to finding Danny.

Being in the crowd felt safe. But feeling safe was a mistake — one I wouldn't have the luxury of making for long.

We turned a corner and found ourselves in front of Shibuya station. I was thankful for the mass of bodies. I felt warm with gratitude for the flashing neon signs. Small comforts from home, I thought. As I basked in the joy of false security, I heard Stephanie gasp. I barely had time to turn around before I felt the hardness of a gun-barrel in my ribs.

I've seen lots of action films. I knew what I was supposed to do in that situation. Walk a few more feet. Spin to face assailant — grab the gunman by the arm, twist into submission. This is what I envisioned myself doing. If only I'd taken that self-defense class I'd sworn I'd get around to taking. I knew I couldn't out maneuver him, but I wasn't going to go down without some sort of fight.

'Keep walking. Don't get on the train and don't turn around.'

I didn't have to turn around to know

who was behind us. I heard the faint Russian accent behind the man's East Coast drawl.

'Where are you taking us?'

'Заткнись!'

I assumed that meant shut-up. 'Are you going to shoot us right here if I don't?' I started to struggle.

'Stop, Jackie. Just do what he says.'

I glanced at Stephanie. I couldn't get a clear read on her expression; I just knew it wasn't terror and that made me angry. Was she working with this guy? Had she let them know we were here?

'What's going on, Stephanie?'

'Just do what he says.'

'Заткнись! Both of you.'

He wasn't treating her like an accomplice but she seemed to know what kind of mess we were getting into. I figured out pretty quickly that Interpol wasn't the only organization she'd been visited by.

Kazlov's thug was rough with us, tightening his grip on our arms if we slowed. If anyone looked on us with concern, he jammed the gun into our ribs, ordering us to smile — three westerners enjoying the sights of Japan.

He pushed us down the busy street through several intersections before we finally turned a corner. A plain white van awaited our arrival. It was nondescript. No make or model. No license plate, nothing to identify it. I couldn't see anyone in the driver's seat but there was another thug leaning against the back-end smoking a cigarette. He had a long scar down his right forearm. He didn't say a word. He just opened the rear of the van and drew a gun. They threw us in the back, bashing my head against the side.

'Watch your head,' thug number one said with a laugh. 'Wouldn't want the poor little sick girl getting a bruise.'

He knew I had chronic leukemia. It infuriated me. I felt invaded — hunted.

He bound our hands and feet while his partner pointed his gun at us. Again I fought. I knew going to a second location was a death sentence. I wasn't going to be taken to the grave quietly. Stephanie didn't fight. She was passive and obedient. I couldn't understand why and immediately suspicion arose.

We were quickly gagged and blind-folded. The last thing I saw was Stephanie being smacked across the face. With my paranoia in over-drive, I wondered if it was part of the act.

They took no care or concern while driving — taking turns violently, slamming on the brakes. We were tossed around the van like ragdolls. I knew I'd be covered in bruises by the time we arrived.

We continued driving for at least an hour. I couldn't hear anything but the muffled sounds of the van on the road and the occasional smack of my elbow on the metal. I used the time to strategize our escape. I hoped Stephanie was doing the same but had to consider the possibility that this might be a set up. If that were the case, she was probably using the time to rehearse her lines. My feelings toward her were vacillating between hate, if she was in on it and guilt if she wasn't.

I wasn't used to feeling guilt. I think guilt is a waste of time. If you've done something you're ashamed of, make it right and move on. But I couldn't do that this time. I found myself almost hoping she knew exactly what we were walking into. I wanted the responsibility to lie with her. I didn't want to be the cause of potentially cutting her life short.

7

We finally arrived at our destination. The driver slammed on the brakes, tapped the gas, then slammed on the brakes again. I heard both men break out into laughter as we hit the back of the van.

They opened the rear doors and pulled me to the ground. Despite my resolve not to, I groaned as I hit the dirt and heard Stephanie do the same.

'Get up!' one of them said as they brought us to our feet.

'Nice drive, huh, ladies?' I couldn't get over his accent, so distinctly Russian with the warm deep tones of a New York native. I felt like I could open my eyes at any moment and be in Brighton Beach.

'Alexei, take them to the warehouse. We wait, they wait.'

I felt a hand tighten around my wrist. I assumed it was Alexei. 'Let's move it,' he said. They unbound our feet and forced us to walk across the gravel. I heard the sound of rusty metal doors opening. I tripped on a ledge that rose from the gravel.

'Clumsy one,' Alexei said. Apparently he considered himself a comedian and clearly enjoyed his job. 'Sit down.'

He threw me in a chair and ripped the tape off my mouth. It burned and I couldn't stop myself from reacting. He tied me to the chair then walked over to Stephanie.

'If you promise to keep your mouth shut I'll keep it off. Don't bother screaming, we're a long way from anywhere anyone can hear you.'

I heard the tape come off Stephanie and a small whimper come from her mouth.

It had been at least 24-hours since I'd taken medication. I knew I could go a day without it, but I wanted to test the waters.

'I need medication.' The sound of my voice shocked me. It was weak and shook. I didn't realize fear had been hiding in my throat. I stuffed it back down and chastised myself. I needed to take fear out of the equation.

'Ahhh, poor little sick girl.'

His mocking patronization irritated me. I hated not knowing how he knew about my illness. I wondered if Stephanie had told them.

'You're an idiot. You clearly aren't authorized to kill us or we'd already be dead and if you don't want me dead you better give me the meds. They're the only thing keeping me alive.' I was being a little dramatic. It wasn't as if I'd die immediately upon missing a day's dose, but I wanted to see where I stood.

His response was a stinging smack to my face and a hatefully spoken Russian word that I was sure did not mean, sure, let me get that for you.

After his tantrum he approached me. I could feel the vibration of his anger as though it was coming from his pores. 'Where are they?' He posed the question in a tone that could've just as easily meant I look forwarding to killing you.

'In my coat pocket.'

He moved toward me. I felt heat from his body. He wrapped his hand around my arm and squeezed. Then he squeezed

252

my thigh a few times before reaching up to fondle my breast. I stayed motionless but my stomach turned in disgust. 'You don't feel like a sick woman. You feel good. Nice and healthy, real nice.'

My face contorted slightly as I cringed and I had to stop myself from spitting on him. For the first time I was grateful for the blindfold. I didn't want to know what he looked like. I didn't want to have to envision his face in my nightmares.

I heard him fumble with the lid and shake the pill into his hand. His willingness to give me the medication encouraged me. I wasn't stupid enough to think he felt sympathy for me. I knew he'd enjoy the opportunity to beat, rape and kill me if given the order. But it confirmed I was right. He was clearly not authorized to kill us. If they'd wanted us dead, we'd already be a memory.

He jerked my face from side to side.

'Open up, sick woman.'

He tightened his grasp on my jaw, forcing my lips apart. He pressed the pill into my mouth then patted the side of my face.

'All better eh?'

The pill was hard and caught in my throat. I heard him walk away. His breathing and footfalls were heavy and obnoxious. I heard the knock and ping of him taking something from a table or shelf.

'Here,' he said gruffly.

Before I could respond I felt the cool rim of a glass bottle at my lips. Burning fluid entered my mouth in a wave. Vodka. Not exactly the beverage of choice when swallowing cancer meds., but for a moment I loved this hateful man. It was just what I needed to take the edge off.

'Thanks,' I said.

'Ah, you like that. You like the Vodka, huh? Good girl.'

'What about your girlfriend. She like the Vodka, too?'

I heard him walking over to Stephanie. But before he reached her the metal doors screeched and clamored open.

'Alexei!' shouted another thug. He then rattled off something in Russian that must have meant stop messing around and get over here, because I heard him stomping away grumbling under his breath.

We were silent for a few moments as we took in the sounds of the abandoned warehouse. It's amazing how your hearing steps up its responsibilities when sight is eliminated. I could hear wind blowing under the metal door and muffled voices getting farther away.

'Stephanie?'

I could feel the tension between us.

'Stephanie, I'm sorry.'

'Shut-up! Just shut up! You are in way over your head.' She spat the words viciously with hatred and authority. I imagined the arguments between her and Danny must have been violent.

'Look, I didn't know Kazlov would have men here.'

'You are so naïve, Jackie.'

'Ahhh, I see. So I guess you did.'

'Of course I did. He has men everywhere. Don't be so stupid. I am never out of their sight. They promised me I wouldn't be.'

'You told me your only interaction had been with Interpol.'

'I know what I told you. Did you believe me?'

She knew I didn't trust her for a second. 'No. But to be honest I really didn't care. I wanted information and the way I figure it, you're the one with the most at stake.' She didn't reply to this comment. It felt good to get in a jab. But she quickly responded with a verbal right hook of her own.

'We should've listened to Danny and gotten out of Tokyo.'

Her words hit me like a strike to the jaw. The heightened hearing I'd been appreciating just moments earlier was suddenly replaced with what felt like helicopters in my ear canals. The only thing I heard for a few seconds was the rush of blood swirling around my head. 'It was Danny? The note?'

It wasn't a snappy comeback but I was truly shocked and sick to my stomach from disappointment. Danny had been right outside our door and I missed him.

'Where did you think it came from? Did you really believe I thought it came from someone who was trying to kill us?' She was still angry but she projected it like annoyance rather than the rage she expressed earlier. I wasn't going to pretend I knew what she was up to or that I knew what she was trying to get me to believe. I just wanted to play her game — let her lead. I needed to keep emotions out of it. I was a novice at covert operations, but I was determined to learn the craft quickly. I clearly had a master before me. I needed to keep her talking.

'You did your job well. I certainly bought your fearful victim act. But believe me, it won't happen again.'

Before she could respond the steel doors opened. The smoke from a cigarette made its way through the air while heavy footsteps collided with the cement flooring. The pounding of the heavy boots was a call to regain composure. I stiffened my body in preparation for what might come next.

8

The man didn't speak. He roughly untied my blindfold. I squeezed my eyes open and shut, trying to clear them so I could see. It was dark outside. A single light bulb attached to a rusted chain hung overhead illuminating the warehouse and casting shadows all around. It was an ominous setting. He walked over to Stephanie and untied her blindfold as well. I could see she was starting to get a bruise from the slap she'd received while getting into the van.

The thug gently caressed her face. It wasn't Alexei or the man who'd snatched us from the street.

'Such a shame,' he said, as he clicked his tongue against the roof of his mouth. He bent down and kissed her cheek. She twisted her head away from his face. In response he took her by the hair, thrust her head back and back-handed her in the same spot her bruise was forming.

Reflex demanded she let out a cry but I think I winced more than she did. She wouldn't look at me and I realized she wasn't panicked. She didn't need my assurance.

'Where's Dmitri?'

He let out a scornful laugh. 'You think Dmitri would come all this way for you? You're trash, you and your sweet little boyfriend. Trash!' He had the same slightly Russian accent as the rest of his crew. And the angrier he got, the more Russian he sounded, as though he added the accent for emphasis.

I couldn't make sense of what was taking place. He recognized the confusion on my face.

'Stephanie, I see your friend looks a little confused. You didn't tell her?'

He clicked his tongue against the roof of his mouth again and made a succession of sounds that were intended to convey condescension.

'Viktor, what do you want?' Stephanie asked without a hint of fear or intimidation.

'What do I want? Let's see. What do I

want? What do I want?' He wound his hand around the back of her chair and slid her violently over to me, slamming us together.'

'You tell me what I want, you little whore!'

'I don't know where he is!' Stephanie shouted

'Don't lie to me!'

'I'm not lying, Viktor. I don't know!'

'Then what are you doing here in Japan, visiting Toshi maybe? How long, huh? How long has your lover been waiting here, eating sushi and rice and hiding out at Toshi's while you slept in my bed?'

She was silent. My body seized with panic. For several seconds I was numb. He knew where Danny was. It was all over. I had to find out if they had gotten to him yet. I tried to play it off as though I were indifferent. I was hoping they'd believe I was after Danny to get my money back. 'I don't want to get into the middle of this little lover's quarrel, but if you already know where he is what do you want from us?'

'Did you hear that Stephanie? Lovers.

Do you remember being my lover?' He ran his thumb over her lips and she closed her eyes as though the memory was too much to bear.

'Enough!' I yelled. 'What do you want from us?'

He turned his head toward me and I saw pure evil. 'I tell you when it's enough! Don't you dare give me orders!' His face was inches from mine. The nauseating scent of liquor and cigarettes filled the space between us. It was one of the many times that night I figured we'd never get out of there alive.

'Viktor,' Stephanie said, sweetly, soothingly, 'we'll help you. Please love, just don't be so angry.'

Suddenly the pet name 'love' didn't sound so irritating. I instantly began feeling embarrassed for trying to coach her through our plan. She clearly knew how to handle herself. She was good. She could put on any emotion or persona she needed. She was in complete control of herself.

'Don't,' Viktor said cooly.

'Don't be that way, Viktor. Try to understand.'

I felt like an audience member, watching the climax of a play. Her face had softened. Her voice was seductive. He wasn't looking at her. He purposely kept his gaze down at his feet and gripped his gun tightly. I realized he couldn't look at her, was afraid to.

'I got scared, love. I wasn't sure what to do. Like a child I ran and hid. I'm so sorry I hurt you.'

At this he looked at her. He was angry again.

He started screaming and waving his gun. 'Of me? Of me? You were scared of me!'

I almost laughed at the irony. He was screaming at her and waving a gun around but couldn't seem to grasp the rationale in her fearing him.

'No, no,' she assured him. 'Not of you.' He looked at her and tilted his head, giving her the OK to continue. 'Of Dmitri, of Danny, the authorities, the whole mess, all of it. I am not as accustomed to this life like you.' She hung her head as if embarrassed by her admission.

'I told you I'd protect you. You didn't trust me.'

'I did trust you, but you couldn't be with me all the time. I felt hunted and Dmitri never trusted me. He always had men following me.' She was pleading with him. Her eyes were searching him, begging him to remember her the way he used to.

'I told you I'd handle it.'

'I know and I should have believed you.'

I couldn't believe what I was seeing. She was actually turning the tide. He was softening.

He caressed her cheek again and kissed her mouth. She didn't turn her head this time. She looked as though she enjoyed it. He pulled away and stared into her eyes. He rested his head on hers.

'But you didn't,' he whispered. 'You didn't believe me,' he said again with a little more authority, as if remembering the pain it caused. 'You didn't believe me. You believed him! That loser drug addict!' Then smack, he slapped her again across the cheek before storming out of the warehouse.

9

With Viktor's abrupt departure we were left in darkness once again. The sun had gone down completely and they didn't bother leaving a light on for us. We sat in silence for a while. It was clear Stephanie wasn't about to explain everything to me and I didn't know where to begin asking. I took the silence as an opportunity to start sorting out possible scenarios that could have led us to this point. I came up with lots of variations but all of them had gaps. I needed answers.

'Running into old boyfriends can be a pain, huh?'

'Cute.'

'Is it?'

'He was never my boyfriend'

'Really. I think he'd be offended by that.' My reliance on sarcasm is a crutch. The more stressful a situation the more sarcastic I seem to get.

'I did what I had to do to stay alive and

give Danny time to run.'

'Oh, so all of that was for Danny's sake? Does Danny know how comfortable you made yourself with his mortal enemies?'

'Whose idea do you think it was?'

I was silenced by this revelation. My brother's willingness to use his fiancée as a means for his escape was sickening. But sadly, I wasn't completely surprised. The lowness to which he was willing to stoop — snitching, stealing, and putting loved ones in harm's way was truly disgusting.

'How touching.'

'Don't judge him. We didn't know what else to do. He knew they'd come after me and it was the only way to keep me alive. We're dealing with the Russian Mafia. There's no honor code. They take whatever they want and they do it brutally, to send a message loud and clear.'

'Why couldn't you go to the cops?'

'You're not that stupid, Jackie.'

She was right — going to the cops wasn't an option. She looked as though she was going to continue but I interrupted her. 'Do you think they're listening to us?'

'Of course. But it doesn't matter. There's nothing they don't know; it's about time you understood this.'

I thought of the magnitude of that. She's never been free from fear, not truly anyway.

'They thought Danny left me for dead. So that's the way I played it.'

'But he didn't? He didn't abandon you?'

'Not exactly; he left, but not without saying goodbye and not without a plan. We both hoped Dmitri would leave me out of it, but Danny knew it was unlikely. He knew Kaslov would do anything to get to him and what better way to get to him than through me. The plan was for me to play it off as though I was so angry with Danny that I'd do anything to get back at him — even help Kaslov.

It sounded like a good plan. One I could imagine Danny coming up with on the fly. I pictured him rushing around their apartment, throwing clothes in a rucksack. I could see him breathlessly explaining his plan, probably stuffing the cash he stole from me into his pockets.

'So Kaslov bought it?' I couldn't imagine Dmitri Kaslov being so gullible.

'Not completely. He had me beaten, of course. I was scared to death. But he wanted to make sure I understood he was in control. I was shocked I came out of that beating alive. I was bruised so badly he kept me in a safe-house while I healed.'

'Didn't anyone miss you? No one came looking for you?'

'Not really. It wasn't the first time I'd been MIA. I've disappeared for days, weeks even, in the past. Especially when Danny needed me. People stop asking questions after they hear your excuses too often.'

Listening to her I realized I had so much to be grateful for. I had so many people in my life that cared for me. I felt bad thinking of Kirk who was probably out of his mind with worry for me at that very moment.

'How did you earn their trust?'

'Don't be silly. You never really earn

their trust; you merely prove your worth. Dmitri never fully trusted me but he needed me and hoped I'd eventually lead him to Danny.'

'So they just kept you, like a prisoner?'

'At first, yes. But I took advantage of it. I like having my enemy at arm's length. It was better than being hunted by the unknown.'

I understood where she was coming from. I understood the relief that comes from being face to face with your greatest fear — to have it exposed. It's easier to attack what's in the light.

She shuddered slightly as she continued. 'Dmitri was terrible,' she said. 'He was short tempered with me, impatient. He wanted to know why Danny wasn't contacting me, blaming me. He threatened my life daily. I gave him information to prove my loyalty. I even led them to a safe deposit box that held some of Danny's money. He'd left the key hidden in a wall in our old apartment. That earned me the right to stop being beaten but he was still distrusting.

'I knew my time was limited. These are

ruthless men. They don't keep you around unless it's absolutely necessary. I got desperate and realized Viktor might be my only hope.'

'Stephanie,' I whispered. 'I think you'd better guard your words.' I played along but I was getting suspicious of how free she was with her tale. It couldn't be safe to share all of this and she'd know that.

'We're not getting out of here anyway, there's no reason to keep secrets from them. They find out everything eventually. As I said, there's nothing they do not know and nothing they'll not do to discover whatever it is they think you're keeping.'

'It's hard to imagine Viktor being the source of hope for anyone.'

'Viktor was different from the others. He had Dmitri's respect. He was loyal and had clearly proven himself. He was treated differently than the other underlings. He was smart and Dmitri listened to him. He wasn't just muscle. And lucky for me, I was his reward for a job well done.'

I was embarrassed by my awe. This

woman was impressive. She turned an almost assuredly deadly situation into a life preserver. I am attractive and have been known to use my looks and my femininity to get what I want, but what she began to explain was a whole different level.

'Viktor wanted me and I knew it was only a matter of time before he requested permission to have me.'

'I'm sure they all wanted you. I'm surprised you weren't on the menu on a daily basis.'

'I was in the beginning. Not Dmitri, of course. He considered me a junkie's leftover piece of trash. But for the first few days the men who made sure I didn't escape all took their turn. Then suddenly it just stopped. I learned later Viktor had found out and had them all beaten.'

'How romantic,' I said sarcastically.

'Yes, I know. You've seen what a monster he can be. Oh, what must you think of me, Jackie? Are you sickened?'

'I don't know. I can't even imagine what you must have gone through. What you must be going through.' I meant it. If

270

her story was true it was sickening. 'I'm disgusted by what they did, not by what you had to do to get through it.'

'I learned to make it work. Don't get me wrong, it was a nightmare from beginning to end but I had to make it work.'

'Did Viktor just keep you, like a slave?'

'No, no, it was all quite civilized.'

I couldn't imagine ever using the word civilized to describe what she experienced. Her poise was unwavering.

'After a couple of weeks things finally settled. Dmitri began focusing on other business and Viktor was left to stay with me in the Penthouse. From there it was easy. I stopped flinching when he'd touch me to escort me around, letting him run his thumb up and down my arm. He would tentatively place his hand on the small of my back, testing to see what my response would be; I would relax into his hand. I eventually began slipping my arm through his when we'd walk and he'd lay his hand over mine.

'He's not a rapist. He wanted me to want him — he didn't want to take me. I told him I was scared of Dmitri and of Danny. I gave him the opportunity to protect me. Most women think giving yourself sexually to a man will win him over. But if you really want a man's loyalty make him your savior. They all want to be John Wayne.'

It was a brilliant insight. I thought of Kirk. The best of him always comes out when he thinks he's protecting me. Even after our divorce he looked for opportunities to ride in on his white horse to rescue me. Unlike Stephanie though, I'm no good at playing the damsel in distress. It's not my style. I always left him falling flat.

'So when was the gig up?'

'It went on for months. Viktor convinced Dmitri of my loyalty, but only to a certain degree. I was free to come and go, but never without a tail.'

'How did you get away?'

'Danny. Well Danny and Toshi. Some of Toshi's associates are talented magicians, specializing in the art of disappearing. Danny had phoned in a few favors.' She paused, and with a voice tainted by disgust she spoke again. 'He'd been hiding out under various aliases all over the country while I shacked up with his enemies. I hated myself.'

'It doesn't sound like you had much of a choice.' I didn't know what to say. She didn't want or need my comfort. She needed to erase and I couldn't do that.

'Would you have done it? Would you have given yourself to a monster to save yourself and your drug addict boyfriend?'

I didn't know how to answer. I couldn't imagine being faced with that decision. In my mind I picture myself being able to fight my way out of any situation. But this wasn't imaginary, what she experienced was real life. I knew she needed me to say yes, that in her shoes I'd have done the same thing so that's what I said. 'Stephanie, I'd have done the same thing. What choice did you have?'

'It just felt so wrong. From the outside it appeared as though I was living a normal life and at times it felt like I was. I was even happy sometimes. The first time I genuinely laughed I locked myself in the shower and cried for an hour from shame. I hated myself for having any enjoyment while living like a prostitute.'

'You weren't living like a prostitute you were living like a prisoner.' I had heard of victim's guilt but was shocked to hear it from someone first hand.

'Do you know people were actually relieved I'd finally freed myself of Danny? It was horrible listening to the way they spoke of him. It broke my heart to agree.'

'No one knew you were basically being held captive?'

'No, because it looked like I was freer than ever. In a way, people thought Danny's drug use and our tumultuous relationship was a prison. People told me how happy they were for me to be free'

'That must have been horrendous.' It was sad to think that living with my brother would be a worse situation than being held prisoner by a crazy Russian mobster. But I can imagine her friends must have hated Danny. I would have if I were in their shoes. He's my own brother and if I'd met her I'd probably have told her to get away from him too.

'Dmitri and Viktor allowed me to have my phone, hoping Danny would contact me. They monitored all my calls — for my own safety, of course.' She laughed sarcastically.

'How did Danny reach you if they were bugging your phone?'

'Danny was able to get to Toshi. He gave him a pre-paid phone and told him to get it to me somehow.'

'And that worked?'

'Actually quite well. I told Viktor I wanted him to meet some of my family. The poor man actually thought we were getting serious. He was thrilled.'

The warehouse was dark so I couldn't see her face but her voice sounded solemn, like an elderly person recounting her life just before her death. I was beginning to realize she had no hope we'd get out of there alive. I had to believe she was wrong.

Occasionally we'd hear voices outside and she'd silence herself. But no one came in. We just sat there tied up, stiff with pain and scared. She eventually continued on with her tale.

'One afternoon,' she said, 'we met Toshi at a little café, like a proper couple. Toshi was brilliant. He told Viktor how lovely it was to see me with someone who was successful and stable, unlike that loser drug-addict.'

I couldn't believe how badly I'd misjudged Stephanie's capabilities. She wasn't kidding when she said she'd been doing this for a while. I recalled my coaching her through our plan and felt a twinge of embarrassment. She must have been amused by my confidence in our plan. I couldn't understand why she went along with it.

'Toshi,' she said, 'slipped me the phone when he hugged me goodbye. Viktor didn't suspect a thing. Later that night he left for a meeting. I knew it was my only chance. By then only one man was watching out for me when Viktor would leave and I could see he was bored with the assignment. It was going to be easy to slip by him. I called the number Toshi had programmed into the phone and was in tears before Danny ever came on the line. I knew the minute he said hello he was sober and in control. He was himself. He told me he was going to Japan and wanted me to meet him there. I left that night and never looked back. I snuck out while Viktor was sleeping and actually felt sorry for him. Can you imagine feeling sorry for that lunatic?'

It was a moving story and I felt sorry for her. But my sympathy was tempered by distrust. There were so many unanswered questions I was still hesitant to believe any of it. Just which version of herself was she selling me?

10

We sat in silence for what seemed like hours. The longer we sat there the more questions began to arise. Her story was touching. And her interaction with Viktor was convincing. If all of it was true, the whole thing was terrifying, but how could I possibly know fact from fiction at this point.

'Stephanie, why didn't you tell me Danny left the note?'

'I don't know. I guess I just didn't know if I could trust you and I didn't know what I wanted to do about it. I was tired of Danny giving me the go ahead to come to him then getting paranoid and changing his mind.'

What could I say to that? I couldn't blame her for doubting me. Why would she trust me? Trust no one. I'm sure she was committed to the same code.

'Why did you agree to go forward with the plan to meet him if he told you to get out? You could have worked harder to convince me we shouldn't go.'

'I don't know, I guess I was tired of running, I want it to end. I hoped that maybe he was just angry because I'd brought you to Tokyo, not because our lives were in danger.'

'Have you been in contact with him this whole time?'

'No, our plan was for me to stay in Shimoda for several months without contact. He instructed me to let the authorities follow me for a while, convince them I was really here for a fresh start. But the minute I realized you weren't Interpol or another government agency I realized our time was short. If you found me Viktor wouldn't be far behind.'

Her explanation seemed plausible but I couldn't risk trusting her. 'How do I know this is true?'

'You don't and does it matter anyway? This is the end. They'll use us to get to Danny then they'll kill us all. It's most likely they've already gotten to Danny and he's dead.' She stated this revelation with little emotion. She was clearly spent emotionally and at the end of her perseverance. 'Maybe that's why I went with you. I knew it was going to be over one way or another. My only hope is he got out of Tokyo in time. Where do you think he'd go next Jackie?'

My heart started pounding. Why would she ask me that knowing Dmitri was probably listening? I couldn't see her face to see if she was leading me or deceiving me. I was silent. I was foggy, suspicious and grieving over the possible death of my brother. I needed to be sharp, emotionless. I didn't want to believe her. I couldn't believe her. I didn't come this far to fail. I couldn't believe how stupid I'd been. Who did I think I was up against?

'How would he know? How could he have possibly known that Kaslov's men were here or that we'd decided not to leave Tokyo?'

'Toshi's connected all over the world. I'm sure one of his guys heard some chatter and sent messengers to Danny. He knew the minute we ended up in Tokyo.'

It sounded plausible but a little too neat. There were missing players. Someone had to be putting this chess game together.

The doors reopened and the light came on. Viktor came in violently with his two thugs. He grabbed the arms of Stephanie's chair picked her up in it and slammed her back down.

'You lying piece of junkie trash. Where will he go if he leaves Japan?'

'I don't know,' Stephanie said shakily.

'Don't lie to me, whore!'

'Viktor, I don't know anymore than you do. You've been listening to us talk. Have you heard anything you didn't already know? He's probably still here.'

'He's not at Toshi's. I sent a man there and now that man is dead and Danny's gone. I will ask you again. Where. Is. He?' He was screaming now. I could see his anger had nothing to do with Danny. This was personal.

'I don't know, Viktor! I don't know!'

He smacked her again then stormed out dialing his phone.

Stephanie and I didn't speak again. I

felt in my gut I was being manipulated and I wasn't going to make it that easy for her. I wanted to believe her. But I couldn't be sure if she was part of their plan, a pawn, or if she was a willing participant. I couldn't afford to trust her. We sat in silence until the metal doors clamored opened, the sound calling us to attention.

11

'It must be your lucky day,' Alexei said. 'An agreement has been made.'

'What sort of agreement?' I asked.

'It doesn't matter, Jackie, it's not going to be in our favor,' Stephanie said.

'She's a smart one, eh? She knows when her time's up.'

They pulled us to our feet. As we were walking out the door, Viktor came in.

'Not her.' His voice was authoritative and commanding. He walked over to Stephanie and coiled his fingers around the back of her neck.

Alexei protested: 'But Dmitri said . . . '

Viktor silenced him, 'Enough! She's not going anywhere. She's not part of the arrangement.' He pulled his gun and covered the two men.

'Take it easy. We leave it to you and Dmitri.'

'What are you going to do with her?' I asked concerned.

'Don't, Jackie,' Stephanie said, her eyes begging me to not say anything else.

'I can't just leave you here with him.'

Viktor laughed at my brazenness. 'You think you have a choice? You don't!' He leaned in and kissed Stephanie on the cheek and ran his hand down the side of her body. She looked disgusted. 'Don't worry,' he said, 'she'll be in good hands.' He aggressively forced her back into the warehouse.

I heard her cry out, 'Viktor please!' before he slammed the metal doors behind them.

Alexei steered me away from the warehouse. 'Where are you taking me?'

'Like I said, it's your lucky day.'

We began walking out into an open field. I felt my stomach turn and I couldn't help but ache over Stephanie. We'd walked about 200 yards when we heard the blast from a shot.

'Nooo!' I fell to my knees and immediately felt nauseous. I shuddered and threw up into the tall grass. I immediately regretted my unwillingness to trust her, but what choice did I have.

'Get up!' I was yanked back to my feet and tried to regain balance. I felt the enormity of what that gunshot meant. Stephanie was dead and Danny didn't even know. I was more determined than ever to get to him. But I wasn't even sure I'd get out of this field alive.

'If you're going to kill me, just do it now.'

Alexei stuck his gun to the side of my head. 'I'd like to, sick woman, but orders are orders.'

'What orders? Dmitri? He's ordered you not to kill me? Why? Where are you taking me?'

'Shut up! You talk too much,' Alexei barked.

Keeping my mouth shut was difficult, but I'd learned a few lessons on this excursion. I wasn't going to win any verbal assaults. I needed to keep my mouth shut and hope for a chance to escape.

We stood in the field for several minutes. Alexei and his partner spoke in Russian, occasionally breaking out in laughter. They behaved as though it was just another day at work, hanging out by the water cooler, passing the time during a long business day.

Eventually an old military Hummer pulled up. The Japanese driver looked nervous. They opened the door and instructed me to climb in. I obeyed.

Alexei barked at the driver: 'Don't screw up!'

'Yes, sir,' the driver said weakly.

I propped myself up against the inside of the Hummer. I was tired, dehydrated and covered in sweat. I had no idea where I was going or how I'd survive the journey, but I had to believe I would. If I could just get some rest, I knew I could keep going.

I'm not sure if I fell asleep or if I passed out; but before I knew it, I was being woken up by the driver.

He gently shook my arm. 'Wake up. You need to hurry or you miss your flight.' He spoke in broken, heavily accented English.

'What? What are you talking about?'

'Here, I help you.' The driver opened the door and helped me out of the car.

He untied my hands. 'I don't know what you did or why you tied up but I don't want any trouble. I just drive, that's it. I just drive you to airport, then you get on plane.' He handed me a backpack and told me to go clean up.

I went into the bathroom and looked in the mirror. I looked like I felt, beat up and bruised. My wrists were badly chaffed from the ropes and the side of my face was swollen from being slammed around in the van.

The bag contained a fresh t-shirt, a washcloth, and a toothbrush, clearly a bag packed by a man. To my surprise my own make-up pouch and wallet were included. It was clear whoever put this bag together was instructed to give me whatever I needed to look presentable enough to get on a plane.

I started the process of putting myself back together when the thought of Stephanie entered my mind. I choked down the sob that threatened to build and I braced myself on the sink. The stakes were getting higher. People were dying. The reality hardened me. I felt a renewed drive build up inside my core. This wasn't over. I was ready to keep fighting. I would not lose.

There was a knock on the door.

'I'll be right out!'

'Hurry, ma'am, we will be late.'

'I said, I'll be right out!'

I needed to get control of myself. Any emotion — sorrow, grief or the rage I was feeling in that moment would be a liability. I was given another day to live, fight and find answers. I wouldn't blow it. I needed to move forward.

I left the bathroom restored. I marched past the driver and headed straight for the Hummer. I postured myself as though I'd paid him for his services. I needed to feel in control of the situation, and gauging from the fear in his eyes it would be easy to intimidate him.

He followed me to the car and got into the driver's seat. Before turning the key in the ignition he turned to me.

He handed me a ticket and my passport and began to plead. 'I just take you to airport. No trouble. Please. I will not be paid if you don't get on plane. I think they are not good men. I will not be alive if you don't get on plane.'

I felt my shoulders relax. I understood I wasn't going to have to fight him. I didn't know him but I already felt responsible for one person's death that day and couldn't survive another. I nodded my head in concession. He drove me to the airport in silence. He pulled up to the curb, parked and helped me out. I thought of the way Stephanie described her public relationship with Viktor — civilized. The whole exchange was civilized. There was no hint of what I'd just endured in the days prior. He handed me the bag, pressed his hands together and bowed gently.

I walked into the airport and got on the plane. I was being sent home.

12

The flight was excruciatingly long. I had too much time to replay events, raise unanswerable questions, and revisit tragedy. I felt trapped with nothing to do but think about what happened. I couldn't even plot my next move. I had nothing to go on and no way to get information until we touched ground. I replayed the last few days over and over in my head. Nothing made sense. I couldn't understand who'd negotiated my release? And as relieved as I was that Danny had escaped Toshi's, I was now back at square one without a clue as to his destination.

The plane landed and I made my way to the gate. As I stepped into the airport a federal agent greeted me. He flashed his badge, and led me by the elbow to a detaining room.

'Great. No welcome home sign or bouquet of roses?' I was certain my sarcasm wouldn't be appreciated but I knew it wouldn't get me shot so I just went with it.

'I just have a few questions, ma'am.'

'I just went through hell, can we do this later?'

'What were you doing in Japan, ma'am?'

'You know exactly what I was doing?'

'We need to know if you spoke with your brother or this woman.' He slid a picture of Stephanie across the table. My heart sank. It was a black and white photo taken in Shimoda. 'She wasn't with him. She was trying to start a life for herself and I destroyed her chance by asking her to help me find Danny.' He seemed uninterested in my response.

'And Mr. O'Hara?'

'I'm sure you already know. I didn't find him.'

'You had no contact with him during your stay?'

'No, I wasn't on a nice little holiday catching up with my brother.' I was in no mood to play his games and he was completely unfazed by my irritation.

'Was Ms. Takeda with you upon your release from the custody of Viktor Patrinkov?'

'No. How did you know Patrinkov was holding me? Are your people responsible for my release? Was Stephanie supposed to be released too?'

'When did you and Ms. Takeda part company?'

He was making it clear that I was not the one conducting the interview. I answered him with bitterness in my voice. 'When she was being marched away for her execution.'

'Ms. O'Hara, are you implying that Ms. Takeda was murdered?' He asked me as though I'd just said she'd run to the grocery store.

I looked him in the eye, and with the coldest steel-hard look I could muster, I answered his question.

'She's dead. He shot her.'

He wrote my statement down in his notebook. 'Who shot her?'

'Viktor.'

'Did you see Mr. Patrinkov shoot Ms. Takeda?'

'No, I heard it.'

'But you did not see him shoot her?'

'Who are you, his lawyer?' My irritation was morphing into anger. 'No, I didn't see her get shot. I saw him drag her away and heard her screaming for him to stop and then I heard a gunshot.'

'Thank you, Ms. O'Hara. We'll be in contact if we have further questions.'

'Wait, what are you insinuating? You don't think he killed her?'

'Thank you, Ms. O'Hara. I have no further questions.'

'But I do. Were you responsible for my release?

'I am not at liberty to discuss that.'

'Why? I just want to know who to thank,' I said, with zero sincerity.

'I am not at liberty to discuss the details of how I came into the knowledge of your captivity or your release.'

I was fuming by this point. 'Who's pulling all the strings? Can you tell me that? Who's sitting back playing God? Are you all being paid for your involvement?'

'You are free to go, ma'am.'

'What about Kaslov and his henchmen?

What are you going to do about what they did to Stephanie, or me or my brother for that matter?'

He'd already gotten up from the table and was heading out the door. He paused with his hand on the doorknob and turned toward me. 'Listen, Ms. O'Hara, do you think we don't have a long list of crimes stacked up against Kaslov and his crew? Do you think that your little story, your little interference with federal and international investigations, will be just the nail we needed for his coffin? You have no idea what a mess you've caused. Your adventure means nothing to us or to anyone else. It was just a waste of time. All you did was bring a high-priced call girl back to her boyfriend and give your brother another opportunity to run and hide.' He'd dropped the professional act. He was angry and irritated, and for the first time since coming into contact with me, seemed like a real person. Realizing he'd let his frustration get the better of him, he turned and left. He didn't give me a chance to speak. He just walked out the door and left me sitting at the table.

Stunned, I stood up and headed out of the room and into the airport. I felt as though I was walking in slow motion. It was like walking through a vat of quick sand. People were bumping into me and I couldn't get out of their way no matter how hard I tried. I eventually made my way to the cab line, dazed and paranoid. I had only been standing there for thirty-seconds when I felt someone brush my arm. I gasped and immediately jerked away.

'Hey, Hey, relax, Irish.'

'Kirk!'

I reached up and threw my arms around his neck.

'Hey, sweetheart, it's ok, it's ok. What's wrong? What happened to you? You look awful. Were you in an accident or something?' He smoothed my hair and kissed the top of my head. 'I've been worried sick about you.'

'I . . . I . . . don't even know where to begin.'

'Come on, let's go. I'll get you cleaned up and get you a nice tall martini and you can fill me in. But if this has anything to do with your brother, I'll tell you right now, I'll not be happy.' He was lovingly scolding me, but I knew my story would turn that sweet reprimand into an all out berating.

He took me by the arm and started leading me toward the parking lot.

'I have a car waiting for us,' he said. 'What were you doing in the cab line?'

I was so tired I couldn't make sense of the question at first. But then it occurred to me that I didn't understand how he knew I'd be at the airport. I looked up at him, confused.

'I was waiting for a cab. I didn't know you'd be here. Why are you here? How did you know to come and get me?'

He hesitated for a split second and then I saw it, that little grin he puts on when he's not telling the whole truth. 'Boy,' he said, 'you must really be out of it. You sent me a text asking me to pick you up.'

'I'm really out of it, but I'm not crazy. I didn't send you a text.'

'I have it right here.'

He pulled out his phone and showed me. Sure enough it was plain and simple.

Coming in tonight. Please pick me up. Flight 1470 from Japan.

My stomach dropped. 'I didn't send that.'

'What do you mean you didn't send it?'

'I didn't send it and you know it.' I stopped walking and took him by the arm. Trust No One, I thought. 'Who sent it?'

'Jackie, you're being ridiculous. It's your number.'

He looked genuinely confused. I had to admit that perhaps I was being a little paranoid, but that grin of his and the fact that I knew I wasn't crazy was causing some doubt. Then I remembered my phone was long gone — Alexei had taken it from me when he kidnapped us.

'Kirk, I don't even have my phone.'

That got his attention. 'What? Why not?'

'It's a long story. But one of Kaslov's men sent that text to you. How would they know to send it to you?'

'Whoa, whoa, whoa, hold on a second. Before we start heading down the road of you accusing me, yet again, of being connected to Dmitri Kaslov, what were you doing with Kaslov's men? Why would they have your phone?'

'So you weren't the one responsible for my release?'

'Your release? From where? What is going on, Jackie?'

I wasn't sure if he was telling the truth or not. At that point I was too near total mental, physical, and emotional exhaustion to care. 'Let me get to bed and I'll fill you in tomorrow.'

'Because you look like hell I'll honor that request, but don't you dare think you're off the hook.'

13

The next morning I filled Kirk in on everything. He yelled, hugged me, yelled some more then hugged me again.

'How could you be so reckless! You could be dying, Irish, do you really feel the need to speed up the process. For crying out loud you're not Lara Croft, you can't fly off to fight bad guys in order to rescue your brother. You run an ad agency not a special forces team.'

His concern seemed genuine. But I was convinced he knew more about the whole situation than he let on. He's always maintained his innocence when it came to his involvement with the less than upstanding members of our global community, but I decided not to push it. I figured playing dumb would give me more access to his contacts than probing him would.

'I know, I know, it was stupid. I'm fortunate to be alive. I will never forgive myself for getting Stephanie caught up in the very thing she was trying to escape.'

He calmed down and put his hands on my arms, rubbing them gently. 'Don't do this to yourself,' he said. 'She got herself mixed up in all of that mess long before you showed up. Do you really think she'd been able to hide from them? Do you really think Danny and she would have run off and found solitude some place — gotten married maybe, had a few babies? No, of course not. She was doomed the minute her and Danny made that stupid plan. And besides, didn't you say that the feds intimated that perhaps she was reuniting with Viktor? Maybe it was all an act. It seems likely.'

'That's what it sounded like he was trying to infer but I'm certain she was shot. I saw the hatred in that man's eyes. He wanted to kill her.'

'Cons are great actors. Maybe that's what they wanted you to think. Maybe they're hoping word gets to Danny that she's dead?'

'No. Impossible.' I had never been so conflicted. I didn't want to believe I'd been so wildly deceived but the alternative would mean Stephanie was dead.

'Just drop it, Jackie. You'll never have all your questions answered. You need to learn to live with the loose ends. Just be grateful you made it out of there alive, and put the whole mess behind you. Let your brother run until he can't run anymore. Let the authorities do their job and bring him in on their own.'

I took a deep breath and weighed my options. I could argue with him. I could beat him down with all my reasons for not just sitting back while my only living relative runs for his life. Or I could smile sweetly and rest my head on the back of the chair and tell him he was right. I decided to go with the second option. I'd learned a little from my trip abroad. Tell people what they want or need to hear and then do whatever it takes to achieve your goal.

I had a whole new list of unanswered questions and I wasn't about to just sit back and leave them unanswered. As soon as I rested, healed, and had time to strategize I'd be back on the road. Kirk could deal with the reality of that another day.

'Okay, Kirk. You win. I guess it's time to call it. I've caused enough chaos.'

'Oh, brother. I know when I've lost. I was married to you remember? I don't believe you for a second.'

'Why, whatever do you mean?' I said with a sly grin.

'You just don't get it do you? This isn't a joke. This will not end well for you, Irish.'

Defensively I perked up. 'At this point I don't care if it ends well, I just want it to end and it can't end until I find him.'

He shook his head, reached for my hand, kissed the back and walked out the door. I knew the conversation wasn't over but it was over for now and for that I was grateful. I would be back on the road soon and needed to get to work. If Danny was still out there I needed to find him no matter where the chase took me.

THE END

We do hope that you have enjoyed reading this large print book.

Did you know that all of our titles are available for purchase?

We publish a wide range of high quality large print books including:
Romances, Mysteries, Classics
General Fiction
Non Fiction and Westerns

Special interest titles available in large print are:
The Little Oxford Dictionary
Music Book, Song Book
Hymn Book, Service Book

Also available from us courtesy of Oxford University Press:
Young Readers' Dictionary
(large print edition)
Young Readers' Thesaurus
(large print edition)

For further information or a free brochure, please contact us at:
Ulverscroft Large Print Books Ltd.,
The Green, Bradgate Road, Anstey,
Leicester, LE7 7FU, England.
Tel: (00 44) 0116 236 4325
Fax: (00 44) 0116 234 0205

Other titles in the
Linford Mystery Library:

NEW CASES FOR DOCTOR MORELLE

Ernest Dudley

Young heiress Cynthia Mason lives with her violent stepfather, Samuel Kimber, the controller of her fortune — until she marries. So when she becomes engaged to Peter Lorrimer, she fears Kimber's reaction. Peter, due to call and take her away, talks to Kimber in his study. Meanwhile, Cynthia has tiptoed downstairs and gone — she's vanished without trace. Her friend Miss Frayle, secretary to the criminologist Dr. Morelle, tries to find her — and finds herself a target for murder!

THE EVIL BELOW

Richard A. Lupoff

'*Investigator seeks secretary, amanuensis, and general assistant. Applicant must exhibit courage, strength, willingness to take risks and explore the unknown . . .* ' In 1905, John O'Leary had newly arrived in San Francisco. Looking for work, he had answered the advert, little understanding what was required for the post — he'd try anything once. In America he found a world of excitement and danger . . . and working for Abraham ben Zaccheus, San Francisco's most famous psychic detective, there was never a dull moment . . .

A STORM IN A TEACUP

Geraldine Ryan

In the first of four stories of mystery and intrigue, *A Storm in a Teacup*, Kerry has taken over the running of her aunt's café. After quitting her lousy job and equally lousy relationship with Craig, it seemed the perfect antidote. But her chef, with problems of his own, disrupts the smooth running of the café. Then, 'food inspectors' arrive, and vanish with the week's takings. But Kerry remembers something important about the voice of one of the bogus inspectors . . .